up a creek

Also by Laura E. Williams

The Executioner's Daughter
The Ghost Stallion

laura e. williams

up
a
creek

henry holt and company • new york

With special thanks to my Southern family—
Lucy, Tim, Madeline, and Logan—
and best wishes to Edy Selman and
her new granddaughter,
who I'm sure is bringing pure joy,
and who I hope grows up to be as smart
and sassy as her grandmother.

Henry Holt and Company, LLC
Publishers since 1866
115 West 18th Street
New York, New York 10011

Henry Holt is a registered trademark of
Henry Holt and Company, LLC

Library of Congress Cataloging-in-Publication Data
Williams, Laura E.
Up a creek / Laura E. Williams.
p.   cm.
Summary: Thirteen-year-old Starshine Bott learns how to cope with an unconventional,
politically active mother and does a lot of growing up in the process.
[1. Mothers and daughters—Fiction.   2. Political activists—Fiction.
3. Coming of age—Fiction.   4. Single-parent families—Fiction.]   I. Title.
PZ7.W666584 Up 2000   [Fic]—dc21   00-57498

ISBN 0-8050-6453-2
First Edition—2001
Designed by Judy Lanfredi
Printed in the United States of America on acid-free paper. ∞
1 3 5 7 9 10 8 6 4 2

Permission to use the following is gratefully acknowledged:
NIGHTS IN WHITE SATIN, words and music by Justin Hayward, copyright © 1967,
1968, and 1970 (renewed), Tyler Music Ltd., London, England. TRO—Essex Music, Inc.,
New York, controls all publication rights for the U.S.A. and Canada. Used by permission.

*For Christy O. and all the other
strong women and girls I have known,
admired, and loved.*

—L.E.W.

up a creek

one

"Raise that poster high, honey," my mama urged, coming up behind me and pushing my elbows in the air. "We need to let the mayor know we mean what we say."

I groaned to myself. My arms ached from carrying the bright orange poster. Miracle (Mama liked me to call her by her first name) had written across it in big black letters, SAVE THE OAKS, SAVE THE SOUTH. I didn't know what saving a bunch of oak trees had to do with saving the South, but Miracle said it was one and the same. Just like she said saving the whales was saving the ocean was saving the earth was saving the people, even though she didn't know if saving people was worth it.

Me, I didn't care much for saving anything. I was burning hotter than a barbecue grill, and all I wanted to do was run through the sprinkler, even if I was too old for such a thing.

"That's my girl," Miracle said, pushing my elbows up a bit higher. "I can always count on you, Starshine." As she swept past, I got a whiff of her perfume. Patchouli. It smelled like dirt, but she said that's why she wore it. Made her feel like Mother Earth. She even looked like Mother Earth, with her long brown hair and the strong, straight line of her shoulders—as if she could carry the world on them. I have the same shoulders, only they don't make me look strong, just wide as a linebacker for the New Orleans Saints.

Seemed like the whole town was around Oak Square that day. Half of us to protest the cutting down of the big, old oak trees, each with its monster limbs twisting and stretching up to the sky. The other half of the town was there to watch. The mayor and the town council wanted to use the land for a new town hall. There were news cameras and reporters asking questions and filming us sweaty folks walking around with posters. Even on the shady side of the square it was hot. Hot, hot, hot.

"Hey, Starshine," Jenna called. My best friend came up and walked alongside me, looking as if she had just stepped out of a refrigerator. With her moon face and doughy body, kids took to calling her Giant Jenna or Jiggling Jenna. But she just laughed her head off like she didn't care one pea pod's worth. I never even saw her cry over it, and I figured that's why we were best friends. Neither one of us had any use for tears.

"Want to carry this for a while?" I asked, waving the poster in front of her face.

Jenna took a step away from me. "Are you kidding? My daddy would kill me if he caught me protesting. He wants to cut down these dumb ol' trees. Says it's progress. And he says your mama—"

"Never mind," I interrupted. I surely didn't need to hear again what Mr. Charbonet thought of my mama. I'd heard it plenty of times before, and I'd sure enough hear it again. Then there was listening to what Miracle had to say about Mr. Charbonet. Him having a Northern heart under that Southern drawl he pretended, and so on.

Jenna looked around and grinned. "If you smile real pretty, maybe you'll make it onto the news."

I bared my teeth at her.

She laughed. "I don't think this town has seen so much excitement since that man broke out of jail and Miss Anna thought she saw him at the Gas Shack pumping high octane into a 1973 Mustang convertible.

Course, the police found out it was only Jeremy Ivy wearing a baseball cap when they pulled him over with their guns drawn."

I shook my head. "I don't know how you remember all those details. That happened three years ago."

"Except for your mama, this town is boring as a flea circus. So when something exciting happens"—she threw up her hands—"I remember it."

"You never remember what's on a math test."

She wrinkled her nose at me. "Math is entirely different, and you know it. Besides, you're not so good at math, either."

I lifted one shoulder. I couldn't argue with that.

"Want to come over and swim later?" Jenna asked.

"Sure I do, only I can't." Sweat trickled down my neck. "I promised Miracle I'd stay here all day."

Jenna shook her head. "It was easier when we wrote those letters to the senators about the baby seals for Miss Miracle."

I nodded. My mama always had a cause, and that meant I had no choice but to have the same cause. And whenever I could, I dragged Jenna into it, too. With one hundred letters to handwrite, it went a lot faster with both of us holding a pen.

"Now she's making you do hard labor," Jenna went on. "I think there are laws against that. Want me to ask my daddy to look into it for you?" she teased, her blue eyes nearly folding up in her face.

"Your daddy doesn't need more business," I said in a grumpy voice, but Jenna knew me well enough to know I was only kidding. "He already represents most of the town. Folks'll have to start suing people from other counties pretty soon 'cause your daddy can't argue against himself in court."

"He'd try if he thought he could get away with it, though," she said with a laugh, walking beside me. I cracked a smile. But pretty soon it slid off my face along with the sweat.

"Now, you're sure you can't come swimming?" Jenna asked one last time.

I imagined the sparkling blue pool the Charbonets built last summer in their backyard, surrounded by azaleas and magnolia trees. Shady and cool. I sighed. "I'm sure."

She shrugged. "See you tomorrow morning, then. Only seven more days of school!"

I waved my poster in good-bye as she walked away. Seven more days and then freedom for two whole months. Freedom, that was, unless Mama latched onto

7

a new cause and dragged me into it. But maybe it'd be something as easy as stuffing envelopes for the Save the Wild Turkey Foundation like we did last summer. Anyway, it'd be summer, and that meant no lessons and no homework and no Mrs. Wermer. Suddenly, the poster seemed lighter and the sun not so hot.

As I rounded the corner, my grandmother came out of the house and made her way across the crowded street, heading right for me. Our house lined up with six others on our side. All together, there were twenty-eight houses that faced Oak Square. The houses were all old, but not as old as the trees, and they had faded wood siding and front and back porches and a pair of scrawny columns holding up the roof over the front door.

"Lordy, it's hotter than the devil's backyard out here," my grandmother said when she reached me. She flapped a delicate hand in front of her face. With her other hand she offered me a tall glass of fresh lemonade.

I scooted out of the way of the other picketers and leaned my poster against my leg. "Thanks, Memaw," I said, before I guzzled half the glass. The sour sweetness tingled just below my ears, and the coldness gave me an instant headache, but it was worth it. I finished the rest in another long swallow. The leftover ice clinked in the glass. I longed to dump the melting chunks down the front of my shirt, but I knew it wasn't proper behavior for a Southern girl. And me, I was born and bred right here in Louisiana, and that made me about as Southern as one can get, which Memaw took no shortage on reminding me.

As though she knew what I was thinking, Memaw snatched the glass out of my hand. She rolled it back and forth against one of her red cheeks, then the other.

I picked up my poster. "You should go inside and sit in front of the fan," I told her.

"I have a pie in the oven and a pile of mending to do. There's no time for lollygagging." When she wanted to, she could be sharp.

"But you look hot and tired," I insisted. "Forget the mending and lie down a bit, why don't you?" I wished I could lie down myself, in a tub of cold water.

"Maybe later."

"Miss Lucy," Miracle said to her mama as she stepped to the side to join us. "What are you doing out in this heat? Are you going to help us picket after all?"

Memaw shook her head. Her closely cropped hair didn't even move.

Miracle waved her arms at everyone. "Isn't it grand? All these people here to help save the oaks?"

Memaw clucked her tongue. "It's a fine thing," she agreed. "But don't mistake activity for achievement."

I saw Miracle clench her teeth, but she didn't say anything back. It was hard to reply to any of Memaw's sayings, and she sure had a drawer full of them.

"Well," Miracle finally said, pushing some of my dark wavy hair behind my ear.

"Well," Memaw said, like she had to finish Miracle's sentence, "I'm going inside. I have to get to that mending, and the house won't dust itself."

Miracle frowned. "I swear there's not one speck of dust in that place. Why don't you put your feet up a bit?"

"What for?" Memaw demanded. "There'll be plenty of time to rest when I'm dead." With that, she marched away, silent in her red shoes and bright white socks. From the back she didn't look like anyone's grandmother.

Miracle and I watched her cross the street and go into our house. Miracle let her breath escape in a loud huff.

"It's a good thing we live with Memaw so we can keep an eye on her. She means it when she says she won't rest till she falls down dead, I swear!"

"Really?" I asked, worrying now that Memaw was out of sight.

"I pray not," Miracle said quietly. Then she brightened. "And what about you? Not going to faint in this heat, are you?"

I grinned. "I don't think so."

"Good." She squeezed my arm before striding off to perk up another sagging picketer.

I lifted my poster, raising it up so everyone could see that if they chopped down these old oak trees, they'd be killing the South as well. I held it high like I meant it, and I walked around Oak Square forty-six more times that day, till all that was left of the sun was a buttery smear in the sky and everyone had gone home except me and Miracle.

two

After our really late supper on account of Miracle being a vegetarian and having to go to the market to get more tofu burgers, she and I sat on the sagging couch in front of the TV. We watched the local ten o'clock news while Memaw washed the dishes in the other room. I sat with a slice of Memaw's key lime pie on my lap. It nearly melted in my mouth. I took tiny bites to make it last longer, enjoying the tingle of sourness right behind my jaw.

"Shhh," Miracle said, "here it comes."

I stopped chewing. Miracle turned the volume up over the clattering silverware and tuneless humming coming from the kitchen.

"The protest continued around Oak Square today, led by Miss Miracle Bott," said the anchorman. I remembered him from when he gave a talk at our school during career week. (Me and Jenna had a bet about the hair on the top of his head.) "With more on the story," he went on in his preacher voice, "here is Luinda Smith. Luinda?"

The camera switched to Luinda Smith who stood in front of an oak tree, a light glaring in her face. "Thanks, Mike. I'm here at Oak Square, so long a place of quiet, now a place of heated controversy. As you can see, the protesters have all left and are probably sitting at home wondering about the fate of the square."

The scene then shifted to earlier this afternoon on the picket line. Miracle grabbed my knee. "Look, Starshine, there you are."

Yep, there I was with my sweaty, frowning face up close on the TV screen. I groaned.

The camera cut to Miracle, looking relaxed and determined. "Destroying these trees is not progress," she was saying into the reporter's microphone. "It's murder. These live oaks have been here longer than this town. They have more right to be here than we do. They give shade and comfort, and they clean the air. What right do we have to destroy them?"

When the scene switched back to the reporter, Miracle let go of my knee. "They cut out the good part," she said. "The part where I said Mayor White is a puffed-up politician who is going to destroy the earth with his progress."

I rolled my eyes. Not that anyone in this town would be shocked by anything Miracle Bott did or said, even on TV. But I often had the feeling my mama forgot she had a daughter named *Starshine*, of all things, in middle school. And no one knew better how to make fun of somebody who had a weird name and a weirder mother than a kid in middle school.

On TV, Luinda Smith said, "Back to you, Mike."

Mike pulled his bushy black eyebrows together like he really cared about this issue. "How do you think this will all work out?" he asked in a concerned tone.

Luinda shrugged on her side of the split screen. "The mayor assured me he's not backing down on this, and the town council has already voted to move forward. I'm afraid there will be no *miracles* here." She grinned at her pun.

The news moved on to a big fire in nearby New Orleans. I flicked off the TV, and Miracle flopped back against the couch.

"You tried," I said.

She snorted. "Not hard enough."

I thought about the hours walking around the square. That felt like hard enough to me.

Memaw, finished with the dishes, stood in the doorway, her hands on her broad hips. "You two look like rag dolls, all floppy and unhappy. What's gotten into you?"

"They're going to cut down the trees anyway," I said, when Miracle didn't look up.

Memaw humphed and scratched a hand through the nearly white spikes atop her head. "What did you expect? Little raindrops will wear down the biggest boulders, but it's not going to happen in one day. Takes time."

"There's no more time left," I said. "It's over."

Miracle stood up abruptly. "Well, you two say what you like, but I'm not giving up on those trees. They need me." She stalked out of the room, leaving behind just the faintest smell of dirt and the sound of her skirt flapping with each step.

I peeked up at Memaw, still standing solid in the doorway. "She won't give up, that one," she mumbled.

"But she has to," I said. "What choice does she have? The mayor said—"

Memaw cut me off with one of her looks. "How old are you?" she demanded.

"Thirteen," I said. I knew what was coming.

"And how long have you known your mother?"

"Thirteen years."

15

"And what's our last name?"

"Bott."

"Now don't you forget it." She went back into the kitchen.

Jenna had heard that exact conversation once and I'd had to explain it to her. But it made perfect sense to me. The only thing I wondered about was if Miracle had gotten married, she wouldn't be a Bott and neither would I, and Memaw wouldn't be able to use that argument. But that's not the way it was.

I got up and went onto the back porch. The rose garden smelled like fertilizer, and the blooms glowed in the light sparkling out through the windows. There were more than one hundred rosebushes in all, and they were Miracle's pride and joy. Every day she weeded them and talked to them, petting their delicate petals with the tips of her fingers.

I sat on the swing, and it creaked softly with each swoosh back and forth. Miracle was up in her room, and I heard her stomping around. Then the Moody Blues floated down, sounding scratchy and old as the album turned on the record player Miracle had bought at a tag sale. She said she liked the sounds of the albums better than the CDs and that nothing should be so perfect.

Nights in white satin
Never reaching the end
Letters I've written
Never meaning to send

I wondered what use there was in writing a letter you never meant to send. All the letters I ever wrote for Miracle—to politicians, to Greenpeace, to oil refineries and other polluting places—were sent right away. Miracle couldn't get them in the mail fast enough.

Memaw appeared on the porch, carrying two glasses of iced tea. She put them on the rickety table and stepped down to the herb garden where she picked a couple sprigs of mint. After she put them in the glasses, she handed one to me, then settled easily on the swing with a small hop. It creaked and groaned in loud protest. I sipped the tea, and the mint tickled my nose. I crushed one of the leaves and inhaled the tangy scent.

Memaw and me sat quiet, rocking back and forth, looking at the roses. My back ached from holding the poster above my head all day. I had known before I started that all that picketing wasn't going to do any good, but I couldn't say no to Miracle. And Miracle couldn't say no to any hopeless cause.

"Memaw, tell me the story," I finally said.

I saw her lips turn up in a soft smile. "That old story?" She knew what story I meant. How many times had she told it? Maybe two hundred? Two thousand?

I took her hand, threading her bony fingers between mine, which were already larger and thicker than hers.

"Mmmm," she murmured, like how she started the story every time. "Your Grampy and me loved each other more than policemen love doughnuts." I giggled at the joke I'd heard so many times. She squeezed my fingers. "We pretended that was enough. We pretended we weren't trying to have a baby, and after so many years, friends stopped hinting about it." She turned to look at me, her face crinkling around her eyes like it always did when she got to this part. "And then, out of the bluest blue came a miracle."

"Miracle," I breathed.

"Forty years old, and I was pregnant. It was a bit of a scandal." She laughed softly. "You just ask Mrs. Bell what a turnaround I gave this neighborhood."

Mrs. Bell was Memaw's age. She lived two houses over and had been friends with Memaw since they were both in diapers. Mrs. Bell told this story almost as good as Memaw.

"And when the tiny red-faced thing was born, Grampy and I didn't even have a name picked out for her. We never really thought it would happen, us having a baby."

I rubbed the back of her hand.

"But the minute I saw her and heard her squalling, I knew it was a miracle. So Miracle's what we named her. And she hasn't stopped squalling since."

We both laughed.

That was Miracle's story. Mine was a lot different. I'd asked Memaw about my daddy before, but I never got much of an answer. I guessed Memaw had some stories she liked to tell, and some she had locked away like Grampy's old revolver. Memaw's hand sweated in mine, but I didn't let go. We rocked until she said she had to finish the ironing.

I went up to bed, waiting for Miracle to come in. She tucked in the sheets so tight, I couldn't even move my feet. When I was little, she used to sing songs she made up as she went along, only I never heard the end of them because I always fell asleep. As I got older, we took turns reading to each other. Right now we were in the middle of *The Secret Garden* for the third time. It was my turn to read, but I knew that when Miracle got caught up in a cause, she did a lot of forgetting. Finally I fell asleep listening to the thump of the Grateful Dead coming from her room.

The next morning the house was quiet.

I opened my eyes to sunlight flooding my room. I tried to stretch my legs, but they could barely move. Surprised, I realized that Miracle must have come and tucked me in sometime in the middle of the night. I hugged Pod, my stuffed purple people-eater that Miracle had given me years ago when I was afraid of the dark. She said that if Pod didn't eat me, I was safe from all other monsters as well.

I wiggled my toes. Monday. After today, only six more days of eighth grade.

I slid out of bed—my lower back still sore—got dressed, and rushed downstairs. Memaw stood at the stove, poaching an egg.

"Where's Miracle?" I asked, surprised not to see her sitting at the table already, searching the morning paper for news. She had to be at Miss Sophie's Magnolia Home for the Elderly in half an hour. That's where she worked. Not that she needed to. "Grampy left us all comfortable," Memaw always said. But Miracle liked the older folks she cared for—reading her own poetry to them, singing, playing cards, and doing art projects. And they signed every one of her petitions to save this, that, and the other thing, even though half of them didn't know what they were signing.

"She's already gone," Memaw said, bringing me my breakfast.

"Where'd she go?"

"I haven't the slightest idea. She wasn't here when I got up."

After breakfast, I trudged off to school. Jenna would meet me at the corner, and we'd walk the rest of the way together. I glanced over at the oak trees. Maybe they'd be chopped down by this afternoon, I thought. They were pretty. I had climbed them and played adventure games amongst them. One of them even had a rope swing, and another held an old tree fort high in its branches. But I wouldn't miss them. Who ever heard of missing a bunch of trees?

three

Before school, the talk was about the dance next week. About how the theme was the Milky Way and how all the girls were getting new dresses.

"The boys can go as aliens," Jenna said, and the small group of girls laughed.

Everyone described the dresses they had or would buy, and then someone said, "Starshine, what about you? Hey, your name goes perfectly with this theme." A few of the girls smiled.

"I'm not going," I said.

Jenna gave me a look. "Yes, you are." Then she turned to the others. "Yes, she is."

I decided to argue with her later. A dance wasn't worth making a stink over.

By fifth period I knew something was going on. Something more than the dance. I'd gotten laughed at before, like when kids teased me about my name, or when Miracle was in the news for something that most folks thought strange. But this was different. This was something new.

Seventh period, Mrs. Wermer stood at the classroom door with her skinny arms crossed, greeting her students as they entered.

I slipped by her and scooted to my seat, keeping my eyes down on my English textbook that had smiling kids on the front cover. Even they looked like they were laughing at me. I didn't glance up till Jenna sat at the desk next to mine.

She leaned over and whispered, "Did you hear?"

My heart double-timed. "About what?"

The starting bell jangled, and Mrs. Wermer stood before us, looking down her long nose. She had sneaked to the front of the room. "Ladies, would you like to share what you're talking about?"

"Yes, ma'am," Jenna said sweetly. "I was just commenting on how nice Starshine looks in that color blue is all."

"Oh, is that all?" Mrs. Wermer raised one black penciled eyebrow like she didn't believe her.

"Nah," said a squeaky boy's voice from the back

of the room, "they was probably talking about Miss Miracle and how she really done it this time."

The class snickered like they all knew what he was talking about.

Mrs. Wermer threw a hard look around the room from behind the slanty glasses she wore. Only she was allowed to make fun. "Mr. Andrew Pike, it's 'they *were*' not 'they was,' and you would do well to keep your lips buttoned for the rest of class."

I couldn't move, but I could imagine Andrew's smirk as he loudly said, "Yes, ma'am!" like he was in the army or something.

I didn't breathe till we got started reading Shirley Jackson's short story "The Lottery." It wasn't my choice to be the center of attention, but sometimes things just seemed to move in that direction. Here I was, in the middle of something again, thanks to Miracle, only I didn't have any idea of what it was. Just like the time when I was seven, Miracle brought me to a fancy luncheon. Ladies dressed in black and white served us salad with almonds and orange pieces. After they cleared those dishes away, they brought us delicate cucumber sandwiches and fresh melon on the side.

Before they served dessert, a tall woman with frizzy hair stood up in the front of the room and started talking about sending money to the poor orphans in Estonia. Only, she had two feathers in her hat and a pretty piece of fur around her collar.

Miracle interrupted the lady every chance she got, asking about the poor animals she was wearing and weren't they important, too? Some man finally came over and asked us to leave. I was mad at Miracle for a week for making me miss the fancy chocolate-covered ice-cream balls they served for dessert.

Now here I was again, knowing that Miracle had stirred up something, but not knowing what. The sack of dread in my stomach grew heavier and heavier as the class went on. I couldn't focus on the lesson, so when Mrs. Wermer asked me a question, I just stared at her like an idiot.

"Aren't you paying attention, *Starshine?*" she asked.

Was it me, or did she always say my name like she had a dead toad in her mouth? "Yes, ma'am," I said.

"Then why can't you answer this simple question?"

"Uh, could you repeat it, please?"

She repeated the question slow and loud, like I was backward. "Why were the town folks excited to go to the lottery even though they knew one of them would be stoned to death?"

It didn't take me more than a second before the

words started rolling off my tongue. "Because people are cruel, and they like to pick on someone, anyone, and they like violence just for the sake of violence, and if everyone joined in on the stoning, no one person could be found guilty."

Mrs. Wermer pressed her lips together before saying, "Isn't everyone guilty of something? Could it be they all deserved to be stoned to death?"

"Yes, ma'am," Jenna jumped in. "In the story they were all guilty of murder. And in some places that's a crime punishable by death. My daddy says so."

The conversation went on from there. I sank lower into my seat, hoping not to be called on again. For once, my hoping helped, and I stayed pretty near invisible for the rest of class.

When the bell rang, I raced out with Jenna right behind me. Only six more days of English. Only six more days of Mrs. Wermer stabbing me with her pointy words.

"I'll see you after school," Jenna called, already halfway down the hall.

I took off in the other direction, trying to pretend I didn't notice anyone staring at me.

Eighth-period social studies seemed to go on forever. At last the final bell rang, and I ran outside to find Jenna. She found me first and grabbed my arm. When I whirled to a stop, she stared into my eyes. "You don't know, do you?"

I shook my head.

She took a deep breath. "It's your mama, Starshine." She took another deep breath, like she'd just run a mile.

"*What*, Jenna? What did she do this time?"

"She climbed a tree."

I stared at my best friend. Then I noticed kids were huddling nearby, sneaking peeks at me. I took Jenna's hand and hauled her down the sidewalk.

"What do you mean, 'she climbed a tree'?"

"That's all I know," Jenna said. "I heard Mrs. Russell telling Mr. Jenkins that Miracle Bott really done it this time by climbing a tree."

I walked faster. Not until we rounded the block did I realize we were being followed. And not by a single spy on a secret mission, but by half of General Lee Middle School. I felt like the Pied Piper of Hamlin, only I wasn't sure if I had kids or rats following me.

Soon enough we reached Oak Square. This afternoon there were even more people around than for yesterday's picketing. All I wanted to do was sneak off to my own house and hide.

But with Jenna holding my hand so that we wouldn't get lost in the crowd, we wiggled between the bodies, worming through the thickest part with "'Scuse me, 'scuse me. Oops, sorry, ma'am. Thank you, sir. 'Scuse me."

Suddenly we were in the front of the crowd, staring up into the branches of one of the biggest and oldest of the oaks. It was the tree that cradled the play fort. The fort had been there for years, and the oak had grown around it. Only, it wasn't the tree or the fort causing this attention.

News reporters from all the local stations, with microphones and cameras and bright lights, shoved one another around the base of the tree. Miracle leaned over the edge of the fort high above and waved.

She called, "And I don't plan on coming down till I have the mayor's firm assurance that these trees will be forever safe."

I realized I hadn't had enough dread in me before to prepare for this. This was like thinking you had a C– and getting a big, fat, stinking F instead.

"I am prepared to live up here for a good long time," Miracle was saying. "I've got boxes of food and water to last more than a week, a sleeping bag, bug spray, books to keep me company, and even a potty bucket."

Everyone laughed. I near died.

Then Miracle spotted me. "Hi, Starshine," she shouted.

The cameras and microphones shifted till they were pointed in my direction. A woman stuck her face close to mine. I recognized her as Miss Luinda Smith, the reporter from last night's news. I could see all the dots of sweat like a beaded mustache on her upper lip.

"Are you Miracle's daughter?" she asked.

Wouldn't have done much good to deny it. I nodded.

"What do you think of your mother living up in a tree like a monkey?"

I bit my lip.

"Honey? What do you think of all this?" Miss Luinda Smith pressed, moving the microphone closer to my mouth.

A man with a shiny bald head leaned down and asked, "Speak up, child. What do you say?"

Suddenly the questions and the heat and the pressing bodies overwhelmed me. I shoved my way through the crowd, across the street, and up the porch stairs, into Memaw's waiting arms.

four

Memaw gave me one of her hugs that reminded me more of an explosion than anything comforting. One second she was crushing my bones and squeezing the breath out of me, and the next second she was releasing me like a spring. *Boing!*

"Inside," she said quickly, hustling me through the front door and slamming it behind her.

That's when I saw reporters headed our way. They were tired of Miracle and were now coming to suck our blood. Only they didn't count on Memaw. No matter how hard they knocked, or how long, she refused to open the door. She tugged me into the kitchen and sat me down at the scarred wooden table.

"I made some rhubarb pie this morning. Hungry?"

"No, ma'am," I said, but even as I spoke my mouth watered just thinking about the tart sweetness in her flaky crust. Memaw served me up a piece as though I hadn't spoken. She also poured some iced tea. Even without fresh mint leaves, it tasted good.

She cut a slice of pie for herself and sat down opposite me. We ate in silence, and somehow I cleaned every crumb off my plate.

Soon enough, the reporters stopped banging and calling to us through the front door. When I looked out the window later, I saw that they had all gone back to circle under Miracle's tree. Hungry wolves waiting for their supper to come down.

Memaw whistled and hummed in the kitchen like her daughter wasn't sitting in a tree and planning on staying up there for as long as it took.

I leaned against the door frame. "Don't you care?"

Memaw slapped the dough on the wooden board, scraped it up, and slapped it down again. "About what?"

"You know what about. *Miracle*."

She didn't speak for a while, just punched that dough around. "She's doing what Miracle does. Ever since I can recall, she's had her a tree or an animal or even a bug to save. I remember when she was only four." Memaw took on that faraway look she got when she was looking back some years. "Little as she was, she half carried, half dragged home a dog that had been hit by a car. The dog wasn't dead, but good as. Miracle wouldn't have nothing to do with putting the creature out of its misery. She insisted on caring for Jack, as she named him, night and day. Me and Grampy didn't have the heart to tell her the dog was going to die." Memaw threw out a short laugh. "But what did we know? Miracle brought Jack back from doggy heaven, one day at a time. And sure enough, if that dog wasn't pregnant! Called her Jackie after that."

"But how can she love a tree so much?" I wanted to know when she finished. "It's just a tree."

Memaw never did answer me. And the more I thought on it, the more confused I got. I loved Memaw and Miracle. I loved Jenna and the pet canary I had when I was little, which was now buried in the backyard. And I could see how Miracle might love a dog back to life. But how could a person love a tree? A tree couldn't love you back. It didn't give hugs or kisses. It didn't play with you or make the best pies in Louisiana.

Miracle would figure this out, I finally decided. Then she'd come home to where she belonged.

By five o'clock, the square had mostly cleared out except for a few reporters. Folks left to get ready for supper. That's when Jenna called.

"You ran away," she said in her nicest voice.

"I just couldn't stand it," I explained, twirling the phone cord around my pinkie. "The reporters followed me home."

"I know," she said. "That's why I left you alone for a while. Do you want to come over for supper? Mama invited you. Your grandmother can come, too, if she likes."

I ran to ask, but Memaw just waved her floured fingers at me and told me to go. She'd throw together a spinach salad for herself soon as she finished putting up some pastry dough in the freezer.

I rushed back to the phone and told Jenna I'd be right over. Memaw's big hugs and slices of pie were fine, but sometimes you just need to be with your best friend. Even if her daddy was Mr. Charbonet.

It only took five minutes to race to Jenna's house. I went out the back door and across the lawns and down a path we'd worn next to Mrs. Bell's vegetable garden. I could have gone out the front door and by Oak Square to get there. That would have taken me only three minutes. But I didn't know how much Miracle could see through all those leaves. I didn't want her calling to me with the reporters nearby.

Breathless, I rang Jenna's door, and she opened it

before it even stopped gonging. She hugged me. "I'm so sorry about your mama," she said. "She must really love those trees."

What could I say?

"She's a little crazy, Starshine, but she sure stands up for what she believes in. Aren't you proud of her for that?"

I stared at Jenna. "Are you kidding?"

"But she's so spontaneous. So radical."

I sighed. "That she is," I agreed. "Memaw always says Miracle should have been alive in the sixties when she wouldn't have stood out."

Jenna lowered her voice. "Well, I wish my parents were more like your mama. They're so predictable."

"I would love predictable," I said with half a smile, but fully meaning it.

In the doorway Jenna's daddy popped his head out above his daughter's. He looked like he'd just combed all the hair from one side of his head over the bald spot on top. I knew it wouldn't stay like that for long. "Coming in, Starshine? Or are you just going to let all the bugs out?"

I laughed politely at his sorry joke. "Howdy, sir," I said, stepping into the foyer. "Thank you for having me to supper."

"It's always our pleasure to have you over. Knock, knock."

Jenna groaned.

"Who's there?" I said.

He grinned. "Gorilla."

"Gorilla who?"

"Gorilla me a hamburger, will you?" Mr. Charbonet didn't wait for me to laugh, he just hopped off quick like a jackrabbit, always in a hurry. Memaw was more like a robin, always fixing her nest and pecking away at things until they were done. And Miracle? Like a dragonfly, I guessed, flitting here and there, all delicate and pretty and hard to catch.

Mrs. Charbonet hurried out of the kitchen, a red-checked apron tied around her plump middle. "Oh, you poor dear," she said. With that, she smothered me in her arms and stroked my back. She smelled like cinnamon toast. Finally she held me away from her and said, "How're you holding up, Starshine?"

"Fine, ma'am," I croaked out. And it was true. If everyone would just leave me alone about it, I would be fine.

She shook her head like she didn't believe me. "If you ever need to talk to someone, honey, you know I'm here for you."

I nodded. She patted me on the head even though I was taller than she was, then she disappeared into the kitchen.

Jenna and I looked at each other, trying not to laugh.

"Supper is served," Mrs. Charbonet called a second later.

I followed Jenna into the dining room.

Far as size and shape went, their house was very similar to ours. But while ours had faded wallpaper where the printed flowers looked more like a memory, Jenna's mama had their house decorated real elegant. Stiff, shiny curtains at all the windows, wallpaper with bumps and bright colors, and furniture that looked like it came straight out of a showroom in New Orleans.

We sat down, and Mr. Charbonet said the blessing, then we put our cloth napkins on our laps and waited till everyone was served before we ate. It was always like that at Jenna's house. So orderly and expected. I pretended I was a part of the family. My mama was head of the PTA, and my daddy was a lawyer helping out innocent people. Nice and normal. Only Mrs. Charbonet wasn't much of a cook. The beans were soggy and the roast too salty.

Usually they played symphony music in the background and talked quietly through dinner about school and work and what Mrs. Whatsit said to Mrs. Whosit but shouldn't have. Tonight, though, the small TV in the kitchen was on. It was set on the counter near the dining-room door so only Mr. Charbonet could actually see it, but we could all hear it plain enough when we stopped talking, which we did when Mr. Charbonet held up his hand for silence.

"Oh, Sam, do we have to listen to that?" Mrs. Charbonet said to her husband, glancing at me.

"Daddy, you promised," Jenna said, also looking at me.

"I just want to hear the news," Mr. Charbonet said. "You don't mind, do you, Starshine? Of course not," he continued without waiting for me to reply.

Half a mouthful of salty roast stuck in my throat as I listened to the local news go on about how Miracle was in one of the trees on account of the mayor wanting to chop them all down.

A reporter asked, "Mayor White, do you think you'll have to resort to extreme measures to get Miracle Bott out of that tree?"

Mr. Charbonet aimed the remote at the TV. I was thankful not to have to listen to any more, but he didn't turn it off—he just turned it up.

"Samuel, please!" Mrs. Charbonet scolded, the pouch under her chin shaking with her distress.

"Miss Miracle Bott is certainly prepared for a long haul in that tree," a woman said.

Then Mama's voice: "I've got boxes of food and water . . . "

"Daddy!" Jenna exclaimed.

Mr. Charbonet waved them quiet.

I had just barely swallowed another bite of roast, and now it fought to come back up as I realized what was coming out of that TV next.

" . . . and even a potty bucket."

My life was ruined.

Mr. Charbonet shook his head and changed the channel. I desperately wished I had stayed home with Memaw. I should have known better. Much as I loved Jenna, I knew her daddy didn't care for Miracle. Seemed like they were always on the opposite sides of every issue.

A different man's voice said, "How could a mother leave her child like that to live in a tree?"

"Your mama made national news," Mr. Charbonet said, finally flicking off the TV. "That was Dan Rather. Miss Miracle is big news this time. Big news."

five

The words kept rolling around in my head all the way home. *Big news.* Is that what Miracle wanted? If it meant saving those oaks, she would say yes, no matter how much she embarrassed me.

At home, I didn't feel like sitting on the porch with Memaw, so I went to my room. I took out a piece of pink stationery and sat down on my bed with a book and my favorite purple pen.

Whenever Miracle went away on a march or to protest in front of the White House, she brought me back a souvenir. Nothing big or expensive, but always "important." A book about the extinction of the white leopard, a 3-D photo of the endangered quetzal, a piece of cement from a building. She said if more people hacked away pieces of buildings as souvenirs, pretty soon we'd have endangered cities instead of endangered rain forests and animals.

But the reason for the purple pen was the best. "Because it's your favorite color," Miracle had said when she gave it to me.

Dear Miracle, I wrote. I chewed the end of the pen. What did I want to say to her?

> *Please come out of that tree. I know you love those trees, maybe even love them more than you love me. But if you care at all for me and Memaw, you will come down as soon as you read this.*
>
> *We need you here. Memaw is getting too old to take care of me all the time. Won't you please come home?*
>
> *Love, Starshine*

I reread my letter. "Pathetic," I said out loud when I was finished. "That's what she'll think—that I'm weak and pathetic." I knew I wouldn't send that letter because when she decided to stay up in that tree even after reading my letter, it would pain me too much to know that she had deliberately chosen the oak over her own family.

I crumpled up the pink stationery and tossed it at the wastebasket. I missed.

Letters I've written
Never meaning to send.

The Moody Blues' lyrics came back to me. Just last night I had thought they were nonsense, but maybe songwriters knew more about real life than I thought.

I turned off my light and stared at the ceiling. Miracle had pasted glow-in-the-dark stars up there. "Starlight for my Starshine," she'd said. She'd even placed them in the shapes of real constellations. The Pleiades, Draco the dragon, Ursa Minor and Major, with the North Star right above my bed. "So you'll always know where you are, where you're going, and how to get home."

I wondered if Miracle could see any stars tonight, but probably all the leaves covered her view. So she had nothing to guide her—not even plastic, glow-in-the-dark stars above her head. No wonder she was stuck up in a tree.

I jumped out of bed and grabbed my art box of colored paper, glitter glue, string, scissors, and tape, and tiptoed into Miracle's empty room. I sat on her bed for an hour, cutting out star shapes in the moonlight. Then

I used the glitter glue to make them sparkle like real stars, stuck each one to a string and taped the strings to the ceiling.

When I left, a warm breeze blew through the room, twisting and rustling the stars, calling Miracle home.

My feet dragged on the way to school the next day. Last night, after dinner, Mr. Charbonet had told me about a lady in Oregon who had lived in a tree for two years. Miracle had been living in the old oak for twenty-four hours, no matter that she had thirty-seven stars hanging from her bedroom ceiling. She was out in the tree, and couldn't see what I'd done. Not till this morning had I realized I should have hung those stars in the tree branches where Miracle could take some notice of them.

When I met up with Jenna, she didn't tell me to hurry up or to smile like Memaw had told me to do. She just let me be miserable. She even stopped me and gave me a hug on the corner of Barber and Downes. Didn't say anything, but we both knew she didn't have to. I hugged her back, but my heart and mind weren't in it. All I could think about was getting to school and facing all those teasing comments and smirks.

The first person to come up to me was Andrew Pike. He blocked my way with his feet spread and his arms crossed against his skinny chest. Blond hair fell over his eyes, which he twitched away with a shake of his head every three words. "Your ma sure put herself in a fix this time."

"Mind your own business," Jenna said.

"Why don't you just butt out, Jenna?" Andrew retorted. "Go jiggle somewheres else."

Jenna rolled her eyes and laughed. "That's really funny coming from a boy short enough to mistake for a mosquito," she bellowed. She put her arm through mine, and we tried to walk around him, but he dodged into our path again and said to me, "Why's she so bent and determined to make a stink over those dumb ol' trees? Don't she know Mayor White's going to call in the National Guard to shoot her down if need be? Ain't no tree worth your life."

Jenna huffed. "He is not going to call in the National Guard. My daddy said so."

"Your daddy don't know everything," Andrew said with a sneer.

"He does, too."

"Well, my pa says the National Guard is on its way right now," Andrew said. "And good riddance."

"Your daddy is stupid," Jenna said hotly.

"At least I have a pa," Andrew shot back, looking at me even though I hadn't said a word yet.

My face flamed.

Jenna steered me away from Andrew, who finally shut up. "Don't listen to him," she said. "He's as dumb as his daddy."

"But it's true," I said, watching the sidewalk pass beneath my feet. "I don't have a father."

"Everyone has a father." She led me up the front steps of the school.

"Only mine didn't care enough to stick around."

I remembered Miracle telling me about my father a long time ago. I was in first grade, and I'd never before noticed that I didn't have a pa, since Grampy was always around.

But that year, Grampy had died. And that year, there was a father-and-daughter lunch at school.

"Starshine," Miracle had said, "you don't have a daddy because—well—because I never got married. I had you when I was sixteen. I was so happy to have you, I didn't care about having a husband. I just knew that me and Memaw and Grampy could raise you up to be the perfect girl you are."

I'd laughed and hugged Miracle, so happy to be perfect.

"So you don't have a daddy. But that doesn't bother you none, does it?"

It didn't bother me then, but what did I know at six? Miracle never asked me that question again, maybe because she was afraid she'd get a different answer.

The bell rang for school to start, and I traveled through the rest of the day as though a patch of fog surrounded me. I pretended I couldn't hear comments behind my back. By fifth period the kids got tired of me ignoring them and mostly left me alone.

I didn't see Jenna again until English class. Mrs. Wermer watched me walk down the hall. As I tried to slip by her, she remarked, "You must be having quite an exciting week, Starshine. Your mother is in the limelight." She said it all with a smile on her lips, but it was easy to see how she really meant it.

When class started, Mrs. Wermer set about passing back papers we had turned in on *Romeo and Juliet* two weeks ago. I had written about the importance of names in the play.

Jenna got her paper back and flashed me the A– written at the top. We grinned at each other. English was our favorite subject, even though the Worm, as we called Mrs. Wermer, was our least favorite teacher.

When I got my paper back, I could only stare at the C grade. I knew my paper was as good as if not better than Jenna's. After all, I had helped Jenna with hers. It was Mrs. Wermer being unfair again. She hated me and did everything to prove it.

All year she had given me marks lower than most of the kids in the class. On tests I got A's until the essay portion where I never got anything higher than a B. It wasn't fair, but this time I wouldn't settle, I decided. After school, I'd demand she change my grade.

I was still angry at the end of class when Sharon Beaudreaux walked over with Suanna and Ellie May. They stood behind her and to each side so that Sharon was the point of the arrow aiming right at me.

"Starshine Bott," Sharon said. "Your mother is something strange. But I just want to tell you"—she motioned to her two friends—"we want to tell you that we think it's a fine thing, her trying to save those oak trees. My mama says if anyone can save them, Miss Miracle can." With that, she flounced away, her two friends close at her side.

"I'll be," Jenna said. "I've never heard that girl say

one nice thing in all my life, and she just paid you a compliment."

The twinges of a smile tickled my lips. I gave in to it. I hadn't smiled all day, and it felt good to stretch those muscles.

By the time the end-of-school bell rang, half of me just wanted to forget the grade on my paper, knowing that nothing I did or said would do any good. The other half, though—the half I didn't much hear from—reminded me what Miracle once said about how no one can hear you if you don't speak up.

I felt like a salmon wading upstream as I fought the current of kids trying to leave the building. Mrs. Wermer was in her class erasing the chalkboard. She looked down her nose at me when I came through the door.

"Miss Starshine, what a surprise."

I hesitated a second, then told myself to just do it and get it over with. I pulled out my English paper. "Ma'am, why did I get a C and Jenna get an A–? My paper was better than hers. Why do you always give me such low grades?" I took a gulping breath of air, and Mrs. Wermer cut in.

"What's wrong with a C?" she asked, wiping a puff of chalk dust off her skirt.

I looked at her in amazement. "It's terrible!"

"C stands for average." She turned back to the board and kept erasing. "Your paper was average."

"But it was way better than Jenna's," I protested, silently apologizing to my best friend, "and she got an A–."

"She deserved that grade, not that other people's grades are any of your business, Starshine." She clapped the erasers, then sat at her desk. "And you deserved a C." She held up her hand when I started to argue again. "For you, your paper was average. Had Jenna, or any other number of children written it, it would have been an A. But for you it was only average."

"What?"

"I realize I haven't been easy on you this year, but I know you can do much better. You have the potential to be a wonderful writer just like your mother."

"Miracle?"

Mrs. Wermer looked up from the papers she was shuffling on her desk. "She is a fine poet, and she certainly started somewhere."

I knew she was referring to the poems Miracle got

published in the local paper and in some magazines and even in one book, but I never knew anyone noticed except for me and Memaw. "You read her poems?" I asked.

"Of course I do." She looked at me. "Didn't she tell you? I was her tenth-grade teacher when I taught at the high school."

"You were my mother's English teacher?"

"I was. And I made her work for her grades, too. No one gets an easy ride in my class."

So this woman knew all about how Miracle had gotten pregnant and dropped out of school.

Suddenly I wanted to be anywhere but here with Mrs. Wermer looking at me, not down her nose this time, but in a way that made me want to cry. And I surely wouldn't do that in front of her. Instead, I quickly excused myself and ran out of the room and out of the school. By the time I reached home, my tears were safely tucked away where they belonged.

I flopped on my bed, my arm trailing off the side, fingers searching for the purple folder. I sat up and pulled it onto my lap. It was stuffed full of paper. My poems on every sheet. I read through them.

Miracle's poems were like dances on the page. Mine were just words strung together.

Miracle always asked to see them, but I knew they weren't good enough. And I would never show them to the Worm. I certainly didn't need a big red C marking each one to tell me they were no good to anyone but me.

When the storm broke later, it wailed and threw itself at our house, like it wanted to knock it down just for fun. Lightning jumped around, crashing into anything it pleased.

I stood at the window, trying to peer through the rain out to the square. "I have to get Miracle," I said. "She'll be afraid."

"She's afraid of nothing," Memaw said, standing next to me, her sweatered arms wrapped together like a pretzel. "You leave her be."

"But she might get struck by lightning."

"Lightning don't strike itself," Memaw said.

Even so, I pushed myself into a too-small green rain-coat. Memaw grabbed me by the hood as I headed for the front door.

"I said to stay here. It's too wild out there for you."

"I have to go. I have to get Miracle and bring her back," I protested, trying to tug away.

Memaw shook her head, but let go of me, and I tore out of the house, into the storm.

The wind pushed me around like I was no more than a slip of paper. A soggy slip of paper by the time I'd raced across the road to stand under the oak tree.

I looked up into the waving branches. Big plonks of rain splattered my face and tried to fill my nose.

"Miracle," I shouted. The wind pushed the word back down my throat so even I couldn't hear my own voice. I tried again. "MIRACLE!"

Her head popped over the edge of the platform. She held a wind-bashed umbrella above her. She shouted down to me, but all I heard was, "Get . . . Starshine . . . drown out . . . "

"What?" I yelled back.

"Go home!"

"Not until you come with me."

"What?" she shouted, cupping her ear.

"Come home!"

"You   know . . . can't . . . that . . . stay . . . these trees."

"We need you!"

"What?"

"MEMAW NEEDS YOU!" I screamed.

She shrugged, like she was sorry she couldn't hear me.

I looked around. "No one's going to cut them down now," I said out loud to myself. "Even the reporters are smart enough to go home in this weather."

I looked up at Miracle. Her lips moved, but I couldn't hear anything with the storm rumbling so loud.

She yelled again. "Go home, Starshine!"

I pointed to her.

One last time she shook her head, then she disappeared from view. I could still see the edge of the battered umbrella.

"MIRACLE!"

Nothing.

"MIRACLE!"

Still nothing.

Minutes ticked by, even though I knew she wouldn't look down at me again.

Finally I went home.

Memaw expected I'd return alone. That's why she only had *one* big towel waiting at the front door when I sloshed back into the house.

I peeled off my raincoat, and Memaw wrapped me up tight as a mummy. We both stared out at the storm.

After a while, Memaw said, "Your mama's gone up a

creek without a paddle, and she just don't know how to get back to us."

"Up a *tree*, Memaw," I said, trying to get my words out through the muffling towel. "She's up a *tree*."

"Same thing," Memaw said under her breath. "She's just looking for that paddle."

The storm crashed and moaned outside. Gusts rattled my windows and whistled through the cracks. I listened for another *kapow!* Every time lightning flashed, my heart thumped with dread, waiting for the instant *kaboom* of the thunder, praying it would stay far away from Oak Square and Miracle. I was so tense, my back ached.

Later, I heard Memaw climb the stairs slow and steady. She worked nonstop all day, and by night she said she felt all of her years. (Only that didn't stop her from springing out of bed at five the next morning.) Halfway up she paused for her *sip of tea* as she called it. I knew it was just her way to catch her breath. She'd been sipping tea a lot more lately.

That night I dreamed about having a tea party with Memaw and Miracle. We were all up in the tree fort, and even in my dream, my back ached.

And it still ached when I woke up.

"Carrying that stupid sign's what did it," I muttered as I stood up and bent forward, trying to stretch out the pain. Wasn't till I stood up that I realized the sun was shining. The storm had blown away. And Miracle? Was she still where I'd left her last night? Or had the wind swept her away, too?

I grabbed some clothes and ran into the bathroom. Combing my hair, I brushed my teeth at the same time, almost sticking my toothbrush in my hair. Then I sat down on the toilet.

I stared at my underwear. Dots of sweat sprang onto my forehead and forearms.

Miracle had told me plenty about this day. About the day when I would become a woman. She had explained everything and even shown me illustrations from a book called *A Woman's Blessing*. But the pictures I'd stared at while Miracle pointed out the ovaries, fallopian tubes, and the uterus weren't me. Those pictures weren't my underwear stained red.

seven

For a long time I just sat there. Panic filled my throat, stuffing up my head. What was I supposed to do? Miracle had gone over and over this with me. We'd practically had period alarm drills.

In the cabinet! I reached forward, fingertips pulling open the door under the sink. A pink box of sanitary pads sat there, waiting for me. I opened the box and pulled out one of the individually wrapped pads. After only a little bit of fumbling I unwrapped it and pulled off the strip of tape.

Clean underwear! I needed a clean pair, but how could I get them?

"Memaw!" I called, knowing I'd have to yell a lot louder if I wanted her attention all the way downstairs in the kitchen, with her humming and clattering around. I'd bust my lungs before she heard me.

Forget that, I decided. Carefully as I could, I scooted back to my room and grabbed a fresh pair of underwear and somehow managed to put them on, pad and all. It seemed like I was wearing a diaper. So this is what it felt like to be a woman.

Miracle had become a woman at thirteen, and three years later she was pregnant with me.

I stared at my face in the mirror. I didn't want to get pregnant at sixteen and drop out of school. I wanted to go to college and do something important.

"Starshine," Memaw called up to me. "Breakfast is ready. Come down now or you'll be late for school."

I got dressed and headed downstairs.

"Now, what's wrong with you?" Memaw asked as soon as she saw me.

"Nothing," I mumbled.

"Who do you think you're talking to, Starshine? I haven't been your Memaw all these years for nothing. Tell me what's wrong."

I couldn't keep it a secret forever. I sighed. "I got my period."

Suddenly Memaw wasn't standing there staring at me anymore. She was bustling over near the stove. "The curse." She tched and shook her head as my heart sank lower. It was even worse than I thought.

"Curse?" I repeated.

"You need your mama now," she mumbled, as though I hadn't said anything.

I wondered if she was talking to me or to herself.

She turned to me. "How would you like some pecan pie for breakfast?"

I stared at her. Pie for breakfast never happened, no matter how many times I begged, so this could only mean one thing. Getting my period was the absolute worst thing that could ever happen, or why would Memaw be offering me some of the best loving she knew how to give alongside a scoop of French vanilla ice cream?

I dropped my head onto my folded arms and groaned.

Memaw rushed over and patted me on the back. "Don't fret. It'll all turn out all right."

"How?" I asked into the tabletop.

"Let's make that a big piece of pie," Memaw said, scooting away from me again. That's when I knew all I'd get from my grandmother was food.

I ate half the slice of pie and none of the scooped ice cream, then I dragged myself off to school. Miracle's tree was already surrounded by reporters, even though she'd been up there for two days. I figured she had made it through the storm. My head low, I kept to the opposite side of the street. I longed to go over and talk to her, but I wouldn't get anything important said with everyone crowding around.

I walked slowly and missed meeting Jenna at the corner, so I trudged on to school alone, barely making it to homeroom by the late bell.

In social studies, the last class before dismissal, we had a substitute. I took out a piece of paper and pretended to read the assignment and take notes, but instead, I wrote a note to Miracle. Actually I wrote fifteen notes, and this is the one I ended up with.

Dear Miracle,
Please come down. I got my period today, and I need to talk to you.

Love, Starshine

There was so much more I wanted to say, but I didn't know how to start.

I folded the note into a little triangle and stuffed it in my pocket as the final bell rang. I hurried out of school without waiting for Jenna and ran to Oak Square. I wanted to get there before a crowd of curious kids clustered around Miracle's tree. It would be bad enough fighting off the reporters.

Sure enough, a few were still camped out under the fort, looking wilted and sweaty. They perked up when they saw me. I pretended they weren't there.

"Miracle," I called up.

Her head popped over the edge. "Hi, Starshine," she called back, smiling and waving. She still looked tidy, not like she'd been living up in a tree for two days and survived a thunderstorm.

I held up the triangle of paper. I knew she'd know what it was because we used to write notes to each other. We folded them and left them under the other's pillow. She wrote funny rhymes that made me laugh, and I drew cartoons of us doing silly things with dialogue bubbles coming out of our mouths.

"Toss it up," she said, holding out her hands.

I tossed and missed. And missed. And missed again.

Finally one of the camera guys took the note and lobbed it up. Perfect shot, right into Miracle's cupped fingers. She unfolded the triangle and read the note. I was waiting for her to jump down out of that tree and hug me and tell me everything was going to be okay.

Instead, Miracle clutched her hands to her chest, the note crumpling there. "Oh, Starshine, you're a woman now. I'm so proud of you!" she shouted.

For one big, fat second I just stood there, my mouth hanging open. That's when I noticed the hum of the camcorders, and I knew two things for dead certain. I'd be on the news again tonight, and Miracle wasn't coming down out of that tree for anything.

eight

Jenna stared at me, her eyes wide as quarters. "She really said that? While the reporters were there?" Her words practically came out in a squeak.

"It's not funny," I said.

"I'm not laughing."

I eyed her sideways. "You're almost laughing, and that's the same thing."

"Am not," Jenna insisted. "I'd never laugh at something so awful."

We sipped iced tea in silence for a couple of minutes on the side porch. The air was muggy and still. Memaw had offered us some blueberry rhubarb pie, but we both decided to wait until after dinner.

"Uh," Jenna said.

I turned to her. "Uh? Uh what?"

She glanced at her watch. "It's almost five."

I frowned. "So?" I had a sinking feeling I knew what this was all about. After all, she was her father's daughter.

"Don't you want to see if it's really on the local news?"

I shook my head. "Now why did I know you were going to say that? Do you really think I want to be humiliated all over again, and on television?"

"But maybe you won't be. Maybe they weren't taping just then. You have to be sure, don't you? No use going to school tomorrow all embarrassed if they didn't show it. All that worrying for nothing."

"Maybe."

She stood up and tugged my hand. She pulled me into the living room and turned on the eighteen-inch set. It popped to life just as the da-dadadada-da-da-dadada news music sounded and they zoomed in on the anchors' smiling faces. How they could smile and read the news at the same time always puzzled me.

"See?" Jenna said, patting my knee with her chubby hand. "Nothing yet."

We watched in silence as the two news anchors talked about a boy from a neighboring town who had disappeared before the storm and was still missing.

63

"How sad," Jenna said.

Then the woman turned to the man. "Mike, what goes up and never comes down?"

My stomach lurched. They had been coming up with better jokes at school!

Mike turned to the camera. "I know. Miracle Bott, that's who."

The buzzing in my ears blocked off his voice. Pretty soon the picture changed to a view up the tree and the floor of the fort, with Miracle's head hanging over the edge.

"That little storm didn't scare me," she was saying.

Then a cut to Luinda Smith. "Right after school, her daughter, Starshine Bott, a student at General Lee Middle School, came for a visit."

Cut to Miracle shouting, "Oh, Starshine, you're a woman now. I'm so proud of you!"

Cut to me with a pale face before I turned and fled.

Cut to Luinda Smith showing her teeth as always. "Back to you, Mike."

Jenna muted the sound. "Oh, God, Starshine," she whispered. "I am so sorry."

"Sorry that it happened or sorry you made me watch it?"

She leaned over and hugged me. "Sorry about every-thing. But"—her face perked up—"on the good side, probably hardly anyone will guess what that was all about."

"Right," I said, my shoulders drooping, "just another weird Bott thing."

"And there's another good thing," Jenna said.

I huffed.

"You're really not that popular at school. Probably not that many people even know who you are."

"Thanks a lot, Jenna."

She tried to keep a straight face, but when she started laughing, I couldn't help laughing, too. Maybe I wasn't popular, but it was hard to stay unknown with a mother like Miracle. Still, Jenna was trying. I had to give her credit for that. Besides, it was easier to laugh than to cry.

"Look!" Jenna said, her attention suddenly on the TV. "They're back at the tree fort." She turned off the mute.

"Mike, we're breaking into the weather report with news from Oak Square. The mayor has just arrived." She pressed her earphone for a moment, then said, "It appears he's here to get Miracle Bott out of the tree."

The camera cut to the mayor marching forward, flanked by two firemen in full gear. One of them lugged a silver ladder. A fire truck sat in the background, its lights flashing.

"Oh, no," Jenna said.

I grabbed her arm. "Come on!"

Memaw called to me, but I didn't slow down. "I'll be right back," I shouted.

We raced out of the house, blazing a trail through the crowd. As we got closer, the reporters recognized me and helped push people aside so that I could get closer. I arrived at the same time as Mayor White.

He only glanced at Jenna and me. But just in case, I tried to hide behind my friend and stay invisible. Mayor White jerked his hand up at the tree and called to the firemen, "Get her down." Then he turned to face the cameras. He was calm and even smiled, as though he were just there to rescue a frightened kitty.

One fireman leaned the ladder against the tree. He had to extend it to its full length, and I wondered how my mama had gotten herself and all that junk up there. And for that matter, who emptied her bucket for her? Where'd she get the umbrella? Was someone helping her?

When the ladder was in place, the fireman climbed up while the other held it steady. We all craned our necks to see what was going on up there, but it was impossible to see with the floor of the fort and all the leaves in the way.

Pretty soon the fireman came back down. Without Miracle.

The mayor pressed his lips together. "Well? Is she coming down?"

"No, sir," the fireman said.

"Why not?" asked the mayor pleasantly, his top and bottom teeth stuck together like they were glued shut.

"She's—she's chained herself to the tree, sir."

"She what? Then cut her down!"

"Cut the tree, sir?"

"No, of course not." He smiled at the cameras. "Just carefully cut the chain that's holding her, and then bring her down. Over your shoulder, if you have to."

The fireman shook his head. "It's not that easy, sir. She has a thick chain and it's very tight. We'd hurt her with the tools we have with us. We'll have to call in for some special equipment. Unless you want us to go ahead with what we have . . . "

Mayor White looked tempted, but instead, he smiled and said, "Of course not. We'll wait for another day." One of his assistants whispered to him, and then he turned to me. "You're her daughter, aren't you?"

So much for being invisible.

I nodded.

The reporters pressed in closer, aiming camera lenses and microphones at me and the mayor.

He bent over slightly. For a second I thought he was

going to put his arm across my shoulders, like we'd been friends for years, but he didn't.

"You don't like having your mama up in that tree, now do you, young lady?"

I shook my head.

"You'd like her to be down here with the rest of us, wouldn't you?"

I nodded.

"Maybe there are a few words you'd like to say to your mother. Maybe she'd listen to you."

"I already tried," I said. The microphones came closer to catch my voice.

"Maybe you could try again?" the mayor asked with a smile.

I didn't smile back. "Miracle, come down, please!" I called up.

Chained to the tree, she couldn't peek over the edge of the fort the way she'd been doing, but her voice did float down. "You know I can't do that, Starshine."

Stubborn as an ant, Memaw often said about my mama. Once I tried to correct her. "It's stubborn as a *mule*, not an ant, Memaw."

"You ever watch an ant?" she said back. "No matter how many times you block its way, that ant will go over it, around it, or under it, and head on in the same direction. Now that's stubbornness. A mule is just plain dumb."

I looked at the mayor. He looked away from me and shrugged at the cameras. "Round one to Miracle Bott," he said, not sounding too happy. "But I certainly won't give up. We'll be back tomorrow. This town does not give in to extreme tactics. We *will* have a new town hall."

I slunk away before the reporters could get interested in me again. Jenna stayed right behind me. As soon as we were free of the crowd, she sighed.

"I do respect your mama," she said, "I just don't understand her all the time. How can she stay up there when you and Memaw need her? Especially since you got your . . . you know, today."

"That's just the way she is." What else could I say when I didn't understand myself? We lived at home with Memaw largely on account of Miracle always insisting on keeping the family together. But with her up a tree . . .

My feet dragged going up the stairs to my house. I'd invited Jenna over to eat, so we both walked in together. There lay Memaw on the floor at the foot of the stairs.

nine

"Oh, my God! Oh, my God!" I said over and over again.

"I'll call my daddy," Jenna cried as she raced off to use the kitchen phone.

I crouched next to Memaw, sure to find her skin as stiff and cold as a statue's. Only, Memaw's skin felt warm under my fingertips. I threw myself around her, begging her to still be alive.

Jenna hurried back. "Daddy's coming with the ambulance," she said. She bent down and put a hand on my shoulder. "Look, she's breathing. She's alive!"

"But why won't she wake up? Wake up," I said, softer in Memaw's ear. "Wake up, please."

It felt like forever till the ambulance stopped outside the house, sirens wailing. I expected Miracle to come charging through the front door. She didn't run in with the ambulance workers, and she didn't come in when Jenna's daddy arrived two minutes later. I kept watching for her when they put Memaw onto the stretcher, took her outside, and loaded her in the ambulance. I climbed in behind her.

Before we sped away, I looked toward the trees. "Miracle!" I yelled. Then I realized she must not know what had happened. "She has to come down from the tree right now!" I begged Jenna and her father. "Memaw needs her!"

"Don't worry, Starshine," Mr. Charbonet said. "I'll go tell your mother. We'll meet you at the hospital."

I nodded, not able to speak. Jenna jumped forward as they were about to shut the door. She hugged me and whispered in my ear, "Don't worry, Starshine, your Memaw has too much work to do to die. You'll see."

She pulled away and I tried to smile. *But what if Memaw had finally got all her work done?* I wondered to myself.

They shut the door, and we pulled away from the curb. Memaw had an oxygen mask over her face, and needles and tubes sticking in her arms.

"Why don't you have the siren on?" I fretted.

"Your grandmother is going to be just fine," the woman said, turning to me.

"What's wrong with her?"

"Mmm, probably a tiny stroke, but mostly heat exhaustion. Older folks have trouble adjusting to the heat. But she'll be okay once we get her hydrated and to the hospital."

I nodded and took Memaw's limp hand between my own. I squeezed it. My heart near jumped out of my chest when the hand squeezed back.

At the hospital, strangers in white whooshed Memaw into a room with curtains around the bed, while the ambulance workers filled out papers before waving good-bye. Nurses and doctors fussed over Memaw for a few minutes, then a nurse with a wide dark face sat down next to me.

"That your grandma, honey?"

I nodded. "Is she going to be okay?"

The nurse smiled. "She sure is. She'll be just fine in a couple of days. We're going to keep her here to rest. Do you have someone to take care of you at home?"

I thought of Miracle on her way here. "My mama," I said.

"Fine," said the nurse. She was about to leave, when Mr. Charbonet and Jenna came in. I looked around for Miracle.

Mr. Charbonet shook his head.

The nurse looked at them, her eyebrows lifted.

"Did you tell her Memaw needed her?" I said.

"I did, Starshine. I did."

My eyes stung. "She probably thought you were trying to fool her to come down out of that tree. I'll tell her. She'll believe me."

"Is there a problem?" the nurse asked Mr. Charbonet.

Jenna's dad took a business card out of his vest pocket and handed it to the nurse. "I'm Samuel Charbonet, Attorney at Law, and this is my daughter, Jenna. We'll take care of Starshine till her grandmother goes home. Nothing to worry about. We're good friends of the family."

The nurse looked concerned, but then another ambulance arrived, and she had to rush off to the next patient.

Mr. Charbonet told me and Jenna to sit and wait while he took care of Memaw's arrangements. When he came back, he motioned us out the door with him and gave his report.

"Your grandmother is resting comfortably now. She wants you to come visit tomorrow evening. I told her I'd bring you."

"Did she ask about Miracle?"

"Afraid not."

The next day, school dragged on slower than ever. All I could think about was Memaw in the hospital alone. And I couldn't help hoping that maybe Miracle had come down out of her tree to go see her.

During lunch I felt something wet squish when I sat down next to Jenna at the table. I stood up, expecting to see Jell-O or pudding left by a seventh-grader, but it was just a smear of red on the bench.

I stared at it, not understanding, when Jenna suddenly pulled me back down. She leaned in close and cupped a hand around her mouth. "Starshine, you're leaking."

"What?"

"*You're leaking,*" she whispered louder. "*Blood!*"

I felt like someone had just punched the air out of me. "You mean my period?"

Jenna nodded.

"Is it on my pants?" I asked.

"Yes, and it's even on the bench a little bit. Didn't you change your pad?"

"This morning I did." Shame and embarrassment burned my cheeks. Yesterday I'd only needed one pad.

"What are you going to do?"

I couldn't answer. I couldn't even move.

When I didn't say anything, Jenna offered to go get the lunch teacher.

I barely nodded.

Jenna left and I imagined the blood seeping through my pants and making a big puddle on the floor. I was so scared I didn't dare move to look. Plus I was afraid if I scootched even one inch, more blood would come out. Now I knew why Memaw called it the curse.

"Starshine?"

The way she said my name, I just knew who it was without even turning. Mrs. Wermer. Another punch in the gut.

Jenna took my hand. The sympathy in her eyes hurt more than my shame. By now, other kids were looking on.

Mrs. Wermer leaned down and whispered in my ear, "Starshine, you wrap this sweater around your waist and hurry on to the bathroom. Jenna will get your gym shorts for you to change into."

I shook my head.

"Now go on."

"I can't," I said. "The seat . . . "

"I'll take care of that." Mrs. Wermer had a bunch of napkins in her hand.

I took the sweater. It was yellow with daisies embroidered around the neck and sleeves. I recognized it right away as the one Mrs. Wermer always kept on the back of her chair or wore over her shoulders even in the heat of summer. I tied it around my waist, but I couldn't get my legs to stand up.

Jenna tugged on my arm.

How was I going to lift my legs over the bench without the whole cafeteria seeing my shame?

"Come on, Starshine," Jenna urged. "Nobody's looking now. A kid just threw up his meatloaf at table three."

I saw that everyone was standing up to see as the nurse led the boy out. Quickly I shifted on the bench, keeping my legs together and bringing them up and over to the other side. When I stood up, I could feel the sweater hitting the backs of my legs. Jenna and I hurried through a side door. At the last minute I turned back and saw Mrs. Wermer nonchalantly wiping the seat where I had been sitting.

Later, in my gym shorts and new underpants and a pad from the nurse (I never knew the nurse kept more than bandages and thermometers in her closets), I took the yellow sweater back to Mrs. Wermer. I had checked every stitch of that thing to make sure there wasn't a dot of blood on it.

Mrs. Wermer was sitting at her desk in the empty classroom, correcting papers with her red pen. She stopped when she saw me in the doorway.

"Everything all right?" she asked.

I nodded. I moved forward and held out her sweater, which she took without even looking at it. But I knew she'd probably examine it later with a magnifying glass. She tossed it over the back of her chair.

"Thank you, ma'am," I said. The words didn't choke me like I thought they would.

Mrs. Wermer pressed her lips together and I guessed maybe it was a smile, but I couldn't be sure. "How's your mother?" she asked.

"Fine."

"She still up that tree?"

"I guess so."

This time I knew for sure it *wasn't* a smile on her face. She shook her head and looked back down at the papers on her desk. I could tell she was about to say something that I didn't want to hear.

"I have to get going," I said quickly as I hurried away.

t e n

After school I didn't even wait for Jenna, but rushed off to find Miracle. There must have been another big news story somewhere, because there weren't any reporters under her tree. Hope fluttered in me. Maybe Miracle was at the hospital with Memaw where she belonged.

"Miracle?" I called up, praying I wouldn't get an answer.

Her head leaned over the side.

My heart dropped. I didn't know if I was sad or mad. And I couldn't tell what Miracle was feeling, either. The oak tree was too tall, the fort too high. Only one thing to do.

I started to climb.

Toe holes and branches to hold on to were easy to find. The only scary part was reaching over the edge of the platform and scrambling up. Miracle grabbed my shirt and tugged, helping me. She tried to pull me into a hug, but I stiffened my shoulders and she let go. I caught my breath and looked around. The sleeping bag was laid out, already dry after the storm the other night. Her potty bucket sat on the other side of the fort, and it looked empty so far as I could see. The rest of a blueberry rhubarb pie filled half a pie plate, wrapped in a plastic bag. Right next to her lay a notebook with a pen hooked in the spiral binding.

"Memaw's in the hospital."

"I know. Mr. Charbonet told me. How is she doing?"

"The doctor said she'd be okay, but she needs you. You have to come down today."

"You know I can't do that, Starshine."

"I'll get a ladder for you," I said, purposely misunderstanding her.

"These trees need me."

Anger spurted up through my insides. "Memaw needs you!"

"Memaw has you, Starshine. These trees have nobody to speak for them except me."

"What about your job then? You're always saying how the old folks at Miss Sophie's love you and need you."

"I arranged all that, Starshine," Miracle said with a wave of her hand. "Emma is covering for me."

The heat of the anger started to melt my insides and brought tears to my eyes, but for nothing would I cry in front of Miracle. I blinked fiercely till I had control over myself.

She didn't say anything for a moment. "Isn't Jenna's family taking good care of you?"

"You love these trees more than you love Memaw. And me." I whispered the last two words to myself.

"Of course not, Starshine."

"Yes you do, or you'd be on the ground where you belong. You're a terrible daughter," I blurted out. My hands were balled so tight that my nails were digging into my palms. I pounded on the rough bark, scraping my knuckles.

"Stop it, Starshine!" she cried when I hit the tree again and again. "You'll hurt yourself!"

"What do you care?"

"You know I care!" She reached for me and tried to pull me into her arms again, but I jerked away.

"Not enough," I said, seeing the hurt flash in her eyes. But I couldn't stop. "All you care about is saving trees or whales or whatever. I wish I lived with my daddy!" I swung over the edge of the platform, half hoping I'd tumble through the branches and break an arm. But I was sure even that wouldn't get Miracle out of the tree. I scrambled down, scratching arms and legs, and landed on the ground with a bone-tingling thump.

I heard Miracle call after me as I ran away. I didn't stop. *Let her scream. Let her scream and cry and hurt.*

But just wishing it wasn't enough. When I got home, I didn't even go inside. I went around the back to the small shed I used to play in when I was little. Now it held the lawn mower, different-sized shears, baskets for the cuttings, and gardening gloves. Pots were stacked on the floor. I grabbed the shears used to clip the hedges alongside the house.

The roses smelled sweet, and I almost lost my nerve. But the hurt inside me ached so bad, I only wanted to hurt back. I tore at those rosebushes with the shears. I didn't try to clip them careful like how Miracle had shown me. I didn't lay the flowers in a flat basket so as not to bruise the petals. I just slashed and cut, and the roses slashed and cut me back. My already-bleeding knuckles got scratched and poked. The thorns dug into my hands and arms, catching on anything they could, tearing, ripping.

I couldn't control the fury inside me. I cut at every one of those rosebushes, wanting to destroy them all.

The tears came, and I couldn't stop them this time. They dripped down my cheeks and off my chin, along my neck and soaked the collar of my shirt. I kept hacking at the bushes. I knew how much Miracle loved them, and I didn't want to leave her a single flower.

When I finished, my arms throbbed from opening and closing the rusty shears. I dropped them on the ground and stared at the mess I'd made. It looked like a battle scene. Bloodred petals scattered the ground. Yellow and pink and purple. Stems lurched from side to side, many not cut all the way through, but enough of their white insides showed for me to know they would die soon, turning brittle and brown, the leaves drying out like scabs.

I looked over the garden and I couldn't understand why the pain inside me didn't go away.

With my key, I went into the house. The cold water on my arms stung. I rubbed my arms clean, but some of the gashes kept bleeding till I pressed tissue against them. The tissue stuck in little red and white dots.

I put on a long-sleeved shirt, even though it was hot outside. I would just tell Memaw it was because of the air-conditioning in the hospital, and maybe she'd believe me.

Before I left, I stepped out onto the back porch and looked at the rose garden again. It still smelled sweet, but there was a sharper scent there, too. A smell that didn't belong. It reminded me of the flowers at Grampy's funeral, all those years ago.

I wanted to bring something to Memaw, so I gathered a bunch of the fallen roses that didn't look too damaged. At the garden sink, I carefully snipped off all the thorns and stuck the stems in a vase filled with sugar water to keep them fresh.

When I got to Jenna's house, she took one look at me and cried out, "Starshine, are you okay?"

I winced, hoping her mother wasn't anywhere nearby. I didn't think I could bear one of her mushy hugs.

"I'm fine," I said shortly.

"You've been crying," Jenna went on.

"No, I haven't," I denied.

"I can tell," Jenna insisted. "You're allowed to cry, you know."

I clenched my teeth. "I wasn't crying."

Jenna scowled. "Why are you lying? I'm only worried about you. You don't have to get mad."

"I'm not mad, and I wasn't crying."

"Fine. If that's the way you want to be." Jenna turned about-face and ran upstairs.

I watched her go, wanting to call her back, but she was gone before I could open my mouth.

Mr. Charbonet drove me to the hospital a little later. I carefully balanced the vase on my lap so that I wouldn't spoil his car seat with a water stain. He came into the lobby with me, but he wouldn't come upstairs.

"I'll just wait here for you, Starshine." He pointed to the sitting area and held up his briefcase. "I have enough work to keep busy for a year. So you just take your time. Which reminds me, did you hear about that turtle that ran away from home?"

I shook my head, eager to get up to Memaw.

Mr. Charbonet rubbed his chin. "I do believe I've forgotten the punch line on that one."

I tried to look disappointed. "Maybe you'll remember it later?"

He nodded. "Go on now," he said, looking thoughtful. "I'm sure it'll come to me."

I took the elevator to the third floor, room 303.

Other than being pale, Memaw looked the same. I ran to hug her, spilling some water on her sheets.

"Don't worry none about that," Memaw said, laughing. "One of the nurses will clean it up for me." She lowered her voice. "It's like having a maid. Enough to drive a person crazy, all the tucking and changing and checking. Grampy always wanted to hire me a cleaning girl, but I wouldn't have it. Now I remember why. Too much fussing."

I put the vase on the side table and kissed Memaw on the cheek.

"You scared five years off me," I said, using one of Memaw's favorite expressions.

"I'm sorry, Starshine," she said. "It must have been a terrible fright to find me like that."

"At first I—I thought you were dead."

"Oh, honey," Memaw said, shaking her head, "it'd take more than a little heat and work to do that."

"Mr. Charbonet says we should get air conditioners in the windows. He says anyone who doesn't have air conditioners in the South is crazy and it serves you right."

"Did he now?" Memaw said, puffing up her thin chest. "Well, that's just fine. The Bott family takes pride in being a little crazy."

"How do you feel? Will this happen again? Do you have to take pills?" All my worries flowed out of me like the insides of one of Memaw's overstuffed pies.

"Now, now," she said, "save your worry for someone who needs it, because it'll do no good here. I'll be fine. Doctor said so. Don't you worry none."

I turned to look out the window so she couldn't look at my face. How could I do anything *but* worry? Did she think it was easy being a Bott? Or fun, just waiting for the next crazy thing to happen?

I sighed, and Memaw patted my hand.

"Can I ask you a question?"

Memaw looked hard at me a second. "Can't hurt nothing to ask," she finally said.

"Who's my father?"

I thought of how I'd told Miracle I wished I lived with my daddy. But the truth of it was that I didn't even know his name.

Memaw's gaze flickered up to the muted TV. "I don't know."

I wasn't really expecting an answer—not from Memaw—but I never, ever expected her to say *I don't know*.

"The roses sure are pretty," Memaw said.

I don't know was still filling up my head so full, it was hard to think.

"They're from our garden," I finally managed.

"I recognized them straight away." She smiled. "Grampy loved roses."

I thought she'd say more, but she started to look sleepy.

There was something else I was wondering about. "Memaw?"

"Mmm?"

"How'd Miracle get the rest of the blueberry rhubarb pie you made the other day?"

She patted my hand. "She's still my little girl, you know."

"You were helping her?"

"Somebody had to. I emptied her bucket for her, too."

"But why? She never should have gone up there in the first place. If you didn't help her, maybe she'd be down by now."

Memaw looked at me like she had to force her eyes to stay open. "Starshine, if I didn't help her, someone else would have. Likely someone's helping her right now, since I'm stuck in here. Lots of people believe in what she's trying to do. They're just not brave enough to face the ridicule and the discomfort."

"Brave? Don't you mean selfish?" I muttered.

Memaw shrugged and her eyelids drooped.

"I have to go now," I said, seeing that I was tiring her out. "Mr. Charbonet is waiting for me downstairs. When are you coming home?"

"Doctor says Sunday morning. Sunday I'll be home and everything will be back to normal."

I nodded, pretending to agree with her. When I left the room, Memaw was staring at the roses with half-closed eyes and a half-moon smile.

eleven

I didn't want to spend extra time with Mrs. Wermer, but I had no choice. I'd hardly slept last night, but at least I'd been in a bed. Miracle had spent her fourth night in the tree fort. Questions I didn't even think I cared about wouldn't leave me alone. Most of the night I listened to Jenna breathe. But the sound didn't lull me to sleep. My mind was too busy, turning.

So when school let out I went back to Mrs. Wermer's class. The room was empty. I should have known a teacher wouldn't hang around on a Friday afternoon.

Just as I turned to go, Mrs. Wermer marched down the hall, her heels clicking like a toy gun.

"Are you looking for me, Starshine?"

"Yes, ma'am," I said.

She sailed past me into the room and sat down at her desk. Even though it was the last few days of school and all the kids knew that grades had been turned in, Mrs. Wermer still assigned work and corrected it, graded it, and passed it back like it mattered. She had a big pile of papers on her desk now, and I could see her red pen tapping impatiently to get at them.

"What is it, Starshine?" she asked me when I didn't say anything after following her into the room.

I stood by the desk and fiddled with a wooden apple she had perched there. She removed it from my fingers.

"I was just wondering, ma'am," I said, trying to force the words out. My face burned. I couldn't look at her. "I was wondering about Miracle and . . . "

She narrowed her eyes at me and leaned back in her chair, folding her hands in front of her mouth.

"What would you like to know?" she asked.

I shrugged one shoulder.

"She was very bright," Mrs. Wermer said. "As I told you, Miracle had a talent for writing even back then. She wrote poetry and short stories, but I'm sure you know all that. In fact, just the other day I found this." She leaned over and opened her lower right drawer and pulled out an old brown file folder.

"I thought maybe you'd like it."

I took the folder and opened it, immediately recognizing the handwriting on all the sheets of paper. Miracle's round letters covered each page. I knew right away what they were. Poems. I closed the folder and stuffed it in my backpack. Later there'd be time to pore through it. Right now I still had one more question that needed asking and answering.

"What about . . . well, who was her boyfriend?"

Mrs. Wermer's eyes flashed open. "You mean . . . ? Oh. I see." She stood up and came around to the front of her desk.

My shoes scraped on the floor. I wanted to race out of there. How could I be so stupid!

"I'm sorry, Starshine, I don't remember."

I turned to go. "It doesn't matter."

I was at the door when she said, "Why don't you ask your mother about this?"

How could I explain to anyone that me and Miracle had talked about how babies are made, about the lifecycle of a star, about the tiniest bug in the endangered rain forest, but not about my father. "I can't," I simply said.

Before I knew it, the Worm was standing next to me. I don't know how I ended up with my nose pressed against her shoulder and her arms around me, but suddenly, that's how it was. She didn't smell of dirt like Miracle, or of flour and yeast like Memaw. She smelled like the little sachet of lavender I kept in my underwear drawer.

"It's okay," she murmured as though I was crying.

It was too much. I didn't want anyone feeling sorry for me, especially the Worm. I pulled out of her arms, which was a mistake because now she could look at me and I couldn't hide.

"You don't have to be just like your mother," she said gently.

"What do you mean?"

She watched me for a long second as though I was supposed to be able to read her mind. But she didn't explain herself. All she said was, "You might try the public library. They keep copies of all the old yearbooks. Might find something there." She didn't add, *something about your father,* but I knew that's what she meant. And I knew she knew that's what I wanted to know.

"Thanks," I said, embarrassed to look at her. I left quickly.

Why hadn't I thought of that? I wondered as I walked the three blocks to the public library. My fingertips tingled as I got closer, like they wanted to wiggle and squirm from nerves and excitement. Would I find a picture of my father?

Inside the cool quiet of the Hoag Memorial Library, I asked the lady behind the desk where all the school yearbooks were kept. She led me to a shelf off to the side, right near the audio books.

The librarian left me and I stared at the spines. The top shelf had years dating all the way back to 1929. Looking at the books right about eye level, I found the year I was looking for.

I took *Bonanza 1987* to a cubical in the back. The cover was stiff, like no one had ever opened it. I examined every page. Photos of faculty. Then photos of the seniors. Then came the sports photos, which I breezed through, until one caught my eye. I was going so fast I had to flip back a couple of pages to find it. I stared. Yep, it was Mr. Charbonet all right. A grin tipped up one side of his mouth, and his hair was shaggy, not like the balding patches he had now. I knew he was older than Miracle, and when I read the caption I understood. *Coach: Mr. Charbonet.* Then I remembered Jenna telling me how her father coached basketball and a few other activities at the high school right after he graduated from law school. It was some tangled mess about whether he really wanted to be a lawyer, but his parents had paid for the schooling and he had a baby on the way. The baby, of course, was Jenna.

I flipped on through the pages till I got to the club photos. I didn't know what I expected to find, but there she was, standing with about ten other kids. Her shirt was tie-dyed, and she held up two fingers in the peace symbol. The caption for the photo was "The National Honor Society."

I squirmed in my seat. She probably could've gone to any college she wanted to. I looked at every face in the group, wondering if my father was in the photo.

The next picture I found of Miracle, she was wearing the same tie-dyed shirt, this time in the Environmental Club. Then in the Backpacking Club and *The Magnolia*—the literary magazine. Obviously they had taken all the club photos on the same day.

I went back and studied the pictures again. That's when I realized Miracle had her arm around someone in the Backpacking Club photo. And he had his arm draped over her shoulders. He was tall, maybe a foot taller than Miracle. His hair looked dark and wavy and touched his shoulders. Was this my father?

"James 'Jimmy' Wallace," read the caption.

Jimmy Wallace. I said the name out loud.

Then another name jumped out at me. *Advisor: Mr. Charbonet.* Mr. Charbonet? I looked closer. He was standing next to Jimmy Wallace.

Keeping my finger in the book to mark the page, I continued through the rest of the clubs, then the choirs and bands. The last twenty pages were candid shots. I found a small photo of Jimmy Wallace sitting on a motorcycle, one leg thrust out to balance the bike, arms folded across his chest, dark glasses covering his eyes. The caption read, "Jammin' Jimmy Wallace."

I touched the picture, like I'd be able to get some vibes from it. Vibes to tell me if he was the one or not. Nothing happened.

I flipped back through the senior photos and found James Wallace right there between Amy Walgrin and Sue Williams. I looked back at the Backpacking Club photo, then closed the book. What had I expected? Something. And why did it matter all of a sudden, after all these years of living without a father? Somehow with Miracle up a tree and Memaw in the hospital, I'd never felt so alone.

I returned *Bonanza 1987* to the shelf and pulled out the 1988 yearbook. I turned to the National Honor Society page. No Miracle. Of course not. She was home with a newborn baby. No time for school. No time for clubs or boyfriends.

After dinner, Mr. Charbonet came downstairs wearing a pair of old jeans with patches on the knees and a raggedy T-shirt with the faint letters of *Hard Rock Café*. I squinted my eyes and tried to imagine him with more hair and fewer lines around his eyes.

"Are you really going out like that?" Mrs. Charbonet fretted.

"Daddy looks fine," Jenna protested. "Better than with those suits and ties nearly strangling him," she whispered to me with a grin. I smiled back, glad our fight was forgotten.

"These are my gardening clothes," Mr. Charbonet said, sticking some leather gloves in his back pocket.

"Yes," agreed Mrs. Charbonet, "but for our garden behind the house where no one can see you."

With a grin and a wave, Mr. Charbonet passed through the front doorway, and I hurried after him, leaving Mrs. Charbonet and Jenna behind. I had asked him earlier if he would help me fix the rose-bushes. He didn't know any of the shortcuts, so we stayed along the sidewalks. He nodded and smiled to all the neighbors and called, "Howdy do," like an old-timer. Everyone waved back. Only Mrs. Bell said anything to me.

"Starshine, how's your Memaw getting on, dear?"

"She's fine. She'll be home on Sunday."

"And your mama?"

"She's fine, too," I said, glad we were beyond her house now so that she'd have to shout to be heard if she wanted to ask me any more nosy questions. And old Southern ladies didn't shout.

When we got to my house, I took Mr. Charbonet around to the rose garden. He stopped and whistled. "Oooeee, you sure made a mess, Starshine. Whatever got into you?" When I didn't answer he pulled on his gloves. "Go get a couple pairs of clippers. This is going to take some time."

I was hoping he'd say everything would be okay and he could fix the rosebushes up like new.

I swallowed the lump in my throat. "Are they all going to die?"

"I think we can save some of them, but I'm not promising."

I knew it was bad when he didn't make a joke of it. I got the clippers and he showed me how to cut off the branches right above a nub. A new branch would grow out of that nub, he told me.

"Watch for the prickers," he warned.

I already knew that, and I had the stiff, sore arms under my long sleeves to prove it. We worked for a time in silence. Every once in a while Mr. Charbonet swore under his breath, and I'd look up to see him dabbing at a new scratch on his arm. I never knew how many one hundred rosebushes were until that night.

When it got too dark to see, I went inside to get us cold lemonade and some pieces of pecan pie that Memaw had left on the pie platter. I brought everything out on a tray. Mr. Charbonet gobbled down his slice, then sat back with his drink.

"No one bakes like your Memaw," he said. He took a long swallow of lemonade. "She'll be home on Sunday, and things will get back to normal."

"How can they?" I muttered. "With Miracle still up that tree . . ."

"She can't stay there forever."

He obviously didn't know Miracle as well as he thought he did.

"The mayor will take measures to get her down," Mr. Charbonet continued. "She can't stop progress."

"The firemen couldn't get her down. She chained herself to the tree," I told him.

"That's what I heard."

"She won't come down till Mayor White promises not to destroy the oaks."

"But the trees have to come down for the new building to go up. I'm on the planning committee. With the grand new town hall right here, it'll bring more business to the shops that are sprouting up just off Oak Square. Real-estate prices will rise and . . . " He looked at me and laughed. "Here I go on and on like everyone else is as excited about it as I am. I suppose you take your mama's view?"

I scratched my fork against the blue flowers on my plate. "I don't know what to think."

"Well, not to worry. A lot of folks are like you, Starshine. They sit back and let things take their course."

That sounded like an insult to me. Like I didn't have enough spine to stand up for what I believed. But I didn't know what to believe! That was the problem. I could see Miracle's point of view, even though I wished with all my heart she'd come down from that tree, but I could also see Mr. Charbonet's point of view. And if the building would be as grand as he said . . . I knew Miracle would say he was just using sugar words to poison my mind. But were sugar words any more hurtful than having a mother who'd rather care for a tree than her family?

I took a breath and said right out what I'd been wondering ever since the library. "Was Jimmy Wallace my daddy?"

twelve

Mr. Charbonet didn't gasp in shock like I thought he might. He just tipped back on his chair and looked at me real long. "Don't you know?" he finally asked.

I shook my head.

"Miracle never told you?"

"No, and I never asked."

"Why now all of a sudden?"

I shrugged. "Never seemed important before."

Mr. Charbonet looked out over the garden. "I'm not the one who should be telling you, Starshine."

"But you did know him, right? You were the advisor for the Backpacking Club when Miracle was in tenth grade, and Jimmy Wallace was a senior."

He nodded and reached up to run a hand over his head like he was remembering all the hair he used to have. "That's right. I knew them both. I even went to school with Jimmy's older brother, Ted."

"Is he my father?" I asked again.

"Only your ma could tell you that." He looked at me squarely. "Jimmy graduated and went off to the north country to live in Alaska."

"But what about Miracle? What about me?"

"They were only kids, Starshine. And I'm not even sure Miracle told him about you. None of us knew she was pregnant till after you were born, and by then, Jimmy was gone."

I sat silent, not knowing what to think or feel. My daddy didn't know about me, and I didn't know about him until now.

"Do you ever hear from him?" I asked.

"Used to, at first," Mr. Charbonet said, no longer looking at me.

"Then why didn't you tell him about me? Tell him he has a daughter back in Louisiana?"

"That's not my right," he said slowly. "There's only one person who can tell your father about you." He paused like he was going to say something important. In the end, all he said was, "You need to talk to your mama about all of this." He stood up. "Let's get back to work before I get so stiff I can't even stand."

"Can you just tell me one thing?"

He eyed me from the edge of the porch.

"Can you tell me where he is now?"

"I'm sorry, Starshine, but I don't remember."

I knew I'd get no more out of him, so I put the dishes away and turned on the outside floodlights. Half the roses were trimmed to small, scraggly branches. Here and there a single branch stuck up a good two feet taller than the rest of the bush. A couple even still had roses on the ends. They seemed so lonely, nodding to each other in the slight breeze. The rest of the bushes looked like victims of a tornado, all twisted and ripped apart.

Mr. Charbonet and I went back to work. We didn't stop until all the bushes were trimmed, the cut branches tied up and put on the curb for tomorrow's garbage pickup, the clippers put away, and the lights turned off. When we walked back, the neighbors were no longer sitting out on their porches.

Back at the Charbonets', Jenna was already reading in bed. I changed into my long T-shirt, and then I slipped under the covers.

Jenna turned off her light. "I'm real sorry about our fight."

"Me too," I whispered back. "I—guess I was crying. I just didn't want anyone to know."

"I'm your best friend, Starshine."

"I know, but you never cry."

After a long moment of silence, Jenna said, "I cry sometimes, I just didn't want you to know because you always seem so strong."

I thought I heard a crack in her voice. "What do you have to cry about?"

"Giant Jenna. Jiggling Jenna." Her voice was tight, and I recognized the same feeling in the back of my own throat.

"Best friends, right?" I whispered.

"Definitely," she whispered back.

A little while later, Jenna fell into her soft snores, but I rolled and turned on the hard mattress. Then I remembered the folder Mrs. Wermer had given me. I quietly dug it out of my backpack and flicked on the tiny bedside lamp. It cast a warm glow over the papers.

I'd been right. They were poems. Pages and pages of them. Some were funny. Some were sad. Most were about love. They were all good, though. Not like the ones she published now, but good enough. I couldn't tell by any grade Mrs. Wermer had left on the sheets of paper. There were no red marks anywhere. I could just tell by how they made me feel. I wondered if any of my poems would ever

be good enough to make anyone feel this way . . .
if I ever took the chance and shared them with someone.

The next morning I helped with the Saturday chores.
After all, "You're part of the family," Mrs. Charbonet
said at breakfast.

Jenna squeezed her face in my direction, like she'd
just eaten a lemon. "Oh, boy," she said, "lucky you. And
lucky me! You can do some of my jobs!"

We dusted and vacuumed and watered the plants.
Mrs. Charbonet sent us out for pastries at the French
bakery around the corner and asked us to stop by at
old Mrs. Hansen's on the way home to give her a bit of
sewing Mrs. Charbonet had done for her.

I didn't mind all the work. At home, Memaw kept
everything so tidy and clean, there wasn't much for
me to do. And I never saw Miracle clean anything
except maybe her jangly silver bracelets. I guess she
was used to having Memaw around, too.

When we got home, Mrs. Charbonet greeted us at
the door. She had changed into a short-sleeved dress
with a magnolia flower print. She took the pastries
from me and put them away in the kitchen.

"Ready, girls?"

Jenna grinned.

"Ready for what?" I asked.

Jenna took my hand. "Mama's going to take us shopping for dresses for the dance."

"Really?" Miracle had never taken me shopping for clothes. That was Memaw's job, and her way was always rushing in and out of stores. But shopping with Mrs. Charbonet would be wonderful.

"Let's be off," Mrs. Charbonet said, draping her purse over her arm.

We drove to Rich's department store. Memaw always took me to Wal-Mart for my clothes. We parked and walked in, winding through the shoes and perfumes and jewelry till we came to the *young ladies' section*, as Mrs. Charbonet called it.

She led us to the rack of formal dresses. I had never seen so many frills, bows, and puffy sleeves.

"Look at this one!" Jenna pulled a frothy blue foam puff from the rack and held it up to her.

"I'm not sure blue is your color," Mrs. Charbonet said with a smile.

Jenna's shoulders sagged, but she put the dress back. Memaw always let me choose any color I liked.

Mrs. Charbonet took a pink dress and held it out for me to see. "Do you like this, Starshine?"

"It has so many bows on it," I said. As soon as the words were out of my mouth I realized how they sounded. "I mean it's pretty," I said quickly, "but I don't think pink's my color."

It took us an hour to look at every dress on that rack. Finally we had a pile to take to the dressing rooms. Or rather, Jenna had a pile of dresses; I had three. Two Mrs. Charbonet insisted I try on, and one I half-liked myself. Half.

Even though I went shopping with Memaw, I realized that I usually chose clothes like Miracle's. If I wasn't wearing shorts and T-shirts, I wore flowing skirts rather than fitted, and blouses with dangly things and unusual prints. None of these dresses had anything that dangled other than shiny glass beads, and most of them were in solid colors.

The short-sleeved dress I half liked was green velvet, and it hung loosely, but the bottom flared out around my ankles when I twirled.

"That's nice," Mrs. Charbonet said to me, "but it's rather plain, isn't it? Why don't you put on the other dresses now?"

Jenna tried on three dresses to my every one, and I heard her mother saying, "Too short," "Too long," "Too frilly—it makes you look chubby," "Much too old-looking for you."

And Jenna said, "But I love it!" to every one.

I tried on the two dresses Mrs. Charbonet had chosen for me. The first one was blue with little yellow flowers.

"That's charming on you," Mrs. Charbonet said.

"It itches," I said.

"But it really looks lovely."

"It really itches."

Mrs. Charbonet sighed. "Try on the other one then."

I changed and came out for inspection again. If Memaw and I shopped like this, her checking and approving everything I tried on, we'd never leave the store. But obviously, this is how lots of families did it because there were other mothers and daughters doing the same thing we were.

Mrs. Charbonet clapped her hands together and rocked back on her little cushioned seat. "Oh, Starshine, you look absolutely beautiful."

Now I knew that was impossible, and I was right. In the three-sided mirror I looked like a flower in bloom.

I was all yellow puffs and ribbons. And the yellow made my skin look green.

I sneezed.

"God bless you," several people said.

I sneezed again.

By the fourth sneeze, I was just getting looks and no more God-bless-yous.

"I think I'm allergic to this dress," I said through my stuffed nose. I sneezed again to prove it.

"What a shame," Mrs. Charbonet said sadly.

"I know," I agreed. "I really liked this one, too."

"You can't sneeze all night," Mrs. Charbonet said. "I'm afraid you'll have to get the green dress after all. Unless, of course, you'd like me to choose a few more for you to try on?"

I shook my head and hurried back into the changing room. I felt a little guilty about faking all those sneezes, but there was no way I'd be caught looking like Miss Buttercup.

I sat with Mrs. Charbonet while Jenna tried on the rest of her dresses. Finally they both agreed on a pink one that actually looked good on Jenna.

On the drive home, Jenna babbled on about the dance I wasn't even sure I wanted to go to, but she was so excited, she didn't even notice my quiet. That was fine with me. The more she talked, the less I had to. And a strange thought came to me. Much as I loved Jenna and her parents, and always wanted to be just like them, for the first time in a long time, I was glad not to have a normal, everyday, try-on-every-dress-and-show-me kind of family.

thirteen

After tuna-fish sandwiches and potato chips, I told Jenna I had to get something from my house.

"What is it?" she asked.

"Oh, just a book I was reading. I'll be right back." I hurried out the front door before she could offer to come with me.

I headed toward my house, but it wasn't for a book. Soon as I got home and let myself in, I grabbed Memaw's bird-watching binoculars and slung them around my neck. From up in Miracle's room, I could look down on the square.

I aimed the glasses at the tree fort, but the leaves were too full and bushy to see through. The heat had chased away all the reporters. I was just thinking I'd sneak under the tree myself to check on Miracle, who was going on her sixth day in the tree, when Mrs. Bell scurried across the street from her house. Using the binoculars, I watched her stand below the fort and call up. I zoomed in on her face so close, I could almost read her lips.

I still couldn't see Miracle, but a minute later, a pail on the end of a rope came dangling down from the fort. Mrs. Bell took something out of it, put something in it, and the pail shot up out of sight. The next second, old Mrs. Bell was hurrying back to her house.

I frowned. Seemed like Memaw was right and Miracle didn't need us after all. People were willing to help her, so there was nothing for me to worry about. I was glad, I told myself. Let someone else do it.

That afternoon the sun blazed down, and Mrs. Charbonet closed the front shades against the glare. Cold air blew through the vents.

"Let's go swimming," Jenna suggested.

"I'm freezing," I said, shivering to prove it.

Jenna gave me a look. "Are you crazy? It's boiling outside. You're just cold because the air is on and you're not used to it."

The thought of floating on my back in the water

sounded good. "Okay," I agreed. After we changed into our suits, I told Jenna I'd be right out.

I went to the kitchen phone. I'd been thinking of doing this since I visited the library. Mrs. Charbonet was outside in the garden, Mr. Charbonet was upstairs in his home office, and I could see Jenna already jumping into the pool. I picked up the receiver and dialed the number for Information.

"What city and listing?"

I said the name of our town. Then I hesitated. "Wallace."

"Do you have a street address?"

"No."

"First name?"

"Uh, no."

The operator sighed. "There are seven Wallaces in that area. Are you sure you don't have a first name or initial?"

I heard Mr. Charbonet walking around upstairs.

"How about James?" Maybe Jimmy was named after his father, I thought.

"Hold for the number, please."

I couldn't believe it. My heart jammed up near my throat.

No more sounds from upstairs. I peeked out the window to see Jenna trying to climb onto a float. No sign of Mrs. Charbonet. I would have seen her wide-brimmed straw hat if she were heading inside.

Taking a deep breath, I dialed the Wallace number. It rang exactly two and a half times before a woman answered.

"Is Jimmy there?" I asked, trying to deepen my voice so I wouldn't sound so much like a kid.

"Jimmy? You mean Jimmy junior?"

"Right."

"Oh, goodness, he doesn't live here. He's way up in Anchorage, Alaska. Who is this?"

I laughed, sounding like a wiggly noodle. "An old friend," I lied. "Could I have his number?"

"What old friend? Do I know you?"

I hung up. It gave me an odd shiver to think that maybe that lady was my grandmother.

Anchorage, Alaska. It was a start anyway.

Outside, the heat slammed into me. Even the water didn't ease the intensity of the broiling sun. But after I scrambled onto a floating mat, I squinted my eyes up to the sky. The bougainvillea and magnolia became crazy patches above me.

I drifted, my hands trailing in the water. At night, I'd be able to see some of the stars. Not as many as on my ceiling at home, but real ones. A North Star that could point the way and keep me headed in the right direction. But what good were stars in the sunshine? About as much good as plastic ones, I figured, or paper ones decorated with glitter and hanging from the ceiling in an empty room.

Jenna quietly rammed me from the side. "I can't stop thinking about the dance," she said. When I didn't answer, she splashed me, and that began the water war.

Sunday morning, I hurried home and got the house ready for Memaw. It was already spittin' clean, but I dusted and vacuumed just to leave fresh marks on the carpets. I was thinking of trying to bake a peach pie when Mr. Charbonet brought Memaw home.

I ran and hugged my grandmother. She felt thinner after a few days on nothing but hospital food. She hugged me tight, then let me go with the usual *boing*.

"I didn't go and die," she said sternly. "So wipe that look off your face."

I quickly blinked my eyes and tried to smile.

She nodded. "That's better. Now, did the Charbonets take good care of you?"

"Yes, ma'am."

Mr. Charbonet cleared his throat. "If there's nothing else you need, Miss Lucy, I'll be on my way."

"You sure have been a mighty big help," Memaw said. "I don't know how to thank you."

"It was my pleasure."

Mr. Charbonet put his hand to his forehead like he was tipping a hat at us, then he turned and left.

Memaw heaved a satisfied sigh and looked around. "It is wonderful to be home. Now I think I'll sit a while on the porch before I get to work. Doctor says I need to rest more. Smell the roses, he said, so I do believe I'll take his advice." She headed for the back door. Before I could warn her, she had stepped onto the porch. I saw her sway. I ran to hold her arm, but she stumbled to a chair and nearly fell into it.

"Oh, my Lord, what happened here? What happened here?" she wailed. "Where are the roses? What happened here?"

fourteen

My heart nearly cracked to hear such pain in Memaw's voice, and I could barely get my words out. "I cut them."

She turned to me, her eyes wide. "You? You did this? Why would you do such a thing?"

"I—I was mad at Miracle. I—"

She turned away from me, shaking her head. "Your grampy raised most of them from seed. Nurtured them like they were his children. Didn't buy them at a garden center like they do nowadays."

I didn't know what to say. I had raged against the roses because Miracle loved them, done it to slash out at her. I'd never meant to hurt Memaw.

I knelt at Memaw's side as she sat in stunned silence. "I'm so sorry. But they'll grow back. Mr. Charbonet helped me fix them. He said most of them will be fine."

Memaw didn't even look at me.

Not knowing what else to say, I got to my feet and left her alone on the porch.

If only I had known, I told myself, I would have left the roses alone. And what would I have done instead to get back at Miracle? Broken all her albums? Smashed the crystal ball she kept on the nightstand by her bed? Ripped her books?

I sighed. The anger that had burned in me that day was now only ashes. All I felt was shame.

I went out the front door. The square was quiet. A couple of people sat on their porches, rocking back and forth, fanning themselves with folded newspapers. If the reporters had been there, more folks would be outside, looking to see what else Miracle would do.

I walked across the street, the pavement hot under my bare feet. They'd softened in school shoes, and it'd take a few weeks to toughen them up.

Under the shade of the oaks it seemed at least ten degrees cooler. Fallen acorns stabbed my soles so I tiptoed through the dirt and grass until I was below the fort.

I stood there for a long time, just listening to leaves rustle and mynahs gab. Miracle started humming "Amazing Grace" like she was in church. Looking up into the branches was like looking into the tallest arches of a cathedral.

When the song ended, I called to her.

She leaned over the edge of the fort so only her head and neck showed. "Starshine!" she called down. She seemed so happy to see me. "How's Memaw getting on?"

"She's okay," I said. "She came home this morning.

"Miracle," I called again, even though she was looking down at me anyway, "I didn't mean what I said before. You're not a terrible daughter."

Miracle sighed. "I expect I am, though. A terrible mother, too, probably. Me sitting up here close to a week trying to save these trees, while you and Memaw struggle on without me."

"It's not so hard. I mean—"

"Oh, I know you can survive without me," Miracle said with a short laugh. "I simply mean it must seem awfully easy to you and the rest of them folks out there for me to climb this tree and sit here."

"I don't think it's so easy," I said. "I think you must miss your bed.

"And . . ." I couldn't bring myself to say it.

"And you and Memaw," Miracle finished for me. "Oh, Starshine, I don't expect you to understand what I do or why. It's just that I try to change what I can, only sometimes it makes me forget other things, like how to be with you. Everything I think I'm doing good for you seems to get messed up in the end.

"Memaw's going to be fine," I told Miracle, changing the subject.

"I know. Mr. Charbonet stopped by to tell me."

I gulped. Had he told her about the roses, too? "Was that all he said?"

"Should there be more?"

I looked at the ground to relieve the crick in my neck. It gave me a good excuse not to look in her eyes.

"Starshine?"

I looked up again. "Who's my daddy?"

Miracle leaned farther over the edge of the platform and reached a hand down to me. I thought she'd tumble out head first, but she caught herself just in time. "Stay there, Starshine, I'm coming down."

She disappeared for a second, then one leg came over, and then the other.

"Do you want me to get a ladder?" I called.

She was hugging a branch so tightly, her voice was muffled when she said, "No, I'll be fine."

I bit my lip as I watched her inch down. Her leather sandal slipped on the bark. I gasped.

She laughed shakily. "If the reporters saw me now, they wouldn't call me a monkey."

My face burned with embarrassment. She had known everyone was making fun of her, but still she had stayed in the tree to protect it.

Miracle stretched out a foot to the next large branch, then eased her weight onto it.

I don't know how it happened. It all went so fast, like one of those old movies where everything is jerky and quick. One second Miracle was balancing on a limb, and the next she was cartwheeling down through the leaves. She landed on the ground with a crack as loud as a snapping branch.

"Miracle!" I rushed to her side.

She opened her eyes a slit. "I just wanted to hug you."

I took her hand, but she winced and cried out. I jumped to my feet and tore through the square and across the street into our house.

"Memaw!" I yelled. I found her in the kitchen. "Miracle fell out of the tree!"

"Oh, Lord," Memaw cried, wiping her floury hands

on her apron. She near ran out the door while I sprinted to the phone.

I prayed the shock wouldn't be too much for Memaw, her just home from the hospital not an hour. I dialed 911, and thought I'd be sick right there by the phone as I explained to the lady what had happened. First Memaw, and now Miracle. My family was falling apart and all the lady on the other end of the line could say was, "Now calm down, honey."

"I can't! She's hurt real bad. You've got to come get her."

"Is she bleeding?"

"No. I don't know. I don't think so, but hurry anyhow."

"An ambulance is on the way," the lady said.

I slammed down the phone and raced back to the tree. Memaw was on her knees beside Miracle, holding Miracle's hand.

"You're going to be just fine," Memaw was saying.

"I know, Mama," Miracle said. I couldn't remember the last time I'd heard her call her mother Mama and not Miss Lucy or Memaw. "Now get me back into that tree before Mayor White shows up with his chain saw."

"Don't talk foolish," Memaw said. "You're going to the hospital."

"But the trees. What about them?"

By now Mrs. Bell and several other neighbors had arrived with the ambulance, looking on to see what crazy thing Miracle Bott had done now. I heard Mr. Thatcher say to someone, "Serves her right for doing such a fool thing."

I whipped around to face him. "What fool thing? Trying to save these trees that no one else seems to care about? Trying to save part of the South because she loves it and she's proud of it? Or trying to climb down the tree to give me a hug?" I didn't bother to wait for him to cuss me out. I turned away to watch over Miracle as they loaded her onto the stretcher and put her in the back of the ambulance. The whole time, she insisted that they let her back up the tree. One of the EMTs stopped me from climbing in after her.

"You stay with your grandmother," he said. "Don't worry, I'll take good care of your mama."

Memaw stood next to me, leaning heavily against my shoulder as we watched the ambulance wail off around the corner.

"Will she be okay?" I asked.

"She'll survive. We Botts always do."

fifteen

"This is getting to be a regular routine. Just call me the Charbonet cab company," Mr. Charbonet joked as he drove Memaw and me to the hospital an hour later.

"And we thank you kindly," Memaw said from the backseat. "I don't know how we'll make it up to you."

"A few tasty pies might do the trick," Mr. Charbonet said, winking sideways at me.

I gave him a small smile, but I was too worried to pay much attention. I'd called the hospital, and they said Miracle was in stable condition. She was pretty banged up and had a broken arm, but there was no sign of internal bleeding or a concussion, so I shouldn't worry about her. I couldn't help it, though.

When we pulled up to the emergency entrance, Miracle was already waiting for us in a wheelchair. The nurse wouldn't let her stand until she'd wheeled her out to the car, even though Miracle said she was fine to walk. But when she stood up to get in the backseat beside Memaw, I saw her stiffen with pain, and she eased real slow onto the seat.

Mr. Charbonet closed the door after her and got in the driver's side. From the passenger's side, I turned to watch Miracle. Her face looked pale except where a purple-and-red bruise was flowering on her left cheek.

I couldn't say anything for a minute. It was so nice to just look at her up close instead of through branches and leaves. I could even smell her dirt perfume.

"I'm sorry," I finally said.

"Wasn't your fault, Starshine," Miracle said. She lifted her good arm to touch my cheek. "I'll be better in no time."

I was afraid she'd say "and up that tree again." It seemed like we all expected her to say it, but no one said a thing the entire ride home.

When we got to our house, I walked upstairs with Miracle. She stopped in her doorway so suddenly, I nearly ran into her back.

125

"Oh, my," she breathed. She stepped into her room. I followed. Brightly patterned material covered the two large windows that faced the front of the house. Her bedspread was made of the same fabric. "Did you do this, Starshine?"

I had forgotten about the paper stars. Now they twirled and sparkled in all the colors of glitter glue I owned.

"Yes," I whispered, not sure if this was a good thing or not.

She reached around and draped her unbroken arm over my shoulders. "I've missed looking at stars. Missed my starshine," she said, but I didn't know if she was really talking about stars or me. That's the problem with having a name like mine. One of them, anyway. Still, I think she liked what I'd done.

She turned to me. "So how does it feel to be a woman?"

I shrugged. "Same, I guess, but different."

Miracle tucked a loose strand of hair behind my ear. I couldn't tell if she knew what I meant by my mixed-up answer.

After she admired the stars a bit, Miracle took a bath. She had to be careful not to get her cast wet, but when she came out of the bathroom, rose-scented steam billowed out with her. Her cheeks weren't quite so pale, and her long hair was wrapped up in her flowered pink towel like a turban. She wore a silk kimono, a tie around her waist keeping it closed.

"Feel better?" I asked. I was sitting on the top stair, just outside the bathroom door.

"Much better," she said. She headed for her bedroom, then turned to look at me over her shoulder. "Coming?"

Instead of getting dressed, Miracle gently sat down on her bed, leaning up against the foam pillows. She closed her eyes and sighed. I sat on the edge of the bed, careful not to jar her.

She opened one eye and looked at me. "I sure did miss you, Starshine."

"Me too," I said, barely getting the words out.

"And the bugs up there." She showed me the dozen red bites on her left arm. "None of them were endangered, that's for sure! I only wanted to be home, sitting on the porch with you and Memaw, sipping iced tea."

"Why didn't you come home then?" I asked.

She shook her head. "Because even though my bed was a hard piece of wood and that storm near scared the bugs right off me, I had to save those trees."

"But Memaw could have died."

Miracle smiled. "Not with you here, Starshine. You're strong and independent. I knew you could handle it."

I looked sideways at her. I'd never thought of myself as strong.

Before I could say anything, Miracle started talking again. "I've been thinking about that question you asked me. I knew the day would come," she said quietly. "And I haven't been avoiding it. At least I haven't meant to," she added hastily.

It took me that long to realize what she was talking about. "I guess I just always hoped I'd be enough for you. Well, me and Memaw.

"It's a long story," she went on.

"You don't have to tell me," I said quickly. "And I didn't really mean what I said about wanting to live with him."

"But you should know about your father. You have a right."

"Tell me later, then," I said. Suddenly it didn't seem as important to know.

But Miracle got up and limped over to the bamboo-and-rattan desk in the corner and pulled open the bottom drawer. She dug through some papers and came back with nothing much that I could see. She sat down and handed me a torn slip of paper.

"What's this?" I asked, looking at the numbers written on it.

She paused real long, till I thought she wasn't going to answer. "It's your father's phone number."

Just then Memaw appeared in the doorway, looking at us from one to the other. I shoved the slip of paper into my pocket.

"What's wrong?" Memaw asked.

"We're fine, Miss Lucy," Miracle said, smiling at me. "Don't worry, we'll all be just fine."

"Of course we will," Memaw said with a snort as if that said it all. "When you're walking uphill, you know you're on the right path. Walking downhill you go too fast. Just think of all we'd miss." With that, Memaw turned and left us alone.

I looked at Miracle, and she looked at me. "Come here," she said, lifting her good arm.

I scootched across the bed until her arm held me against her warm body.

"Well," she said into my hair, "if we have to walk uphill, at least we'll have each other to lean on when we get tired." Then she groaned. "Oh, no, now I'm beginning to sound like Memaw!"

We both laughed, and at first I didn't hear the deep rumbling outside. To think of Miracle being anything like Memaw was certainly something to laugh at. But the rumbling finally took over the room, and even the bed seemed to shake. I scrambled to my feet and ran to the window, pulling aside the curtain. Moving more slowly, Miracle stood behind me and stared over my shoulder down to the street below and beyond to the square. A yellow monster filled the road and men in hard hats with ropes hanging from their belts and chain saws in hand strutted around like roosters.

I looked at Miracle. She stared through the glass, not saying a single word of protest. But in her watery eyes, I saw the reflection of all those trees.

I turned and ran and didn't stop when she called after me.

Most of me wanted to stay there with Miracle, cuddling like we were best friends, but a part of me needed to be outside to see what progress really meant. Progress that would make this town better like Mayor White and Mr. Charbonet promised it would.

It seemed like the whole town had come out to see the defeat of the trees. Jenna found me in the crowd and gripped my hand. I saw other kids from school, too. Andrew Pike was trying to climb the tractor. I smiled when a man swatted at him like he was no more than a gnat.

It felt like a carnival instead of the funeral I'd always

imagined. No one looked sad or worried or scared. All around me, neighbors called to one another, smiling and joking, filling the air with noise. But nothing was louder than the chain saws. As soon as they revved up, that's all I could hear.

Jenna and I watched as at least twelve men started cutting down the trees. They began up high, sawing through branches so that they creaked and groaned, then snapped free and crashed to the ground. Limb by limb, the men cut.

Finally the big monster machine rolled in and pushed and pulled the trunk over, spraying dirt as broken roots sprang free of the earth. I hoped Miracle wasn't watching.

"This is terrible," Jenna said, all the laughter gone from her voice.

"It's progress," I said.

We squeezed hands as they started on another tree. And then another and another. Where once there were only cool shadows, now the sun beat down, glaring, making my eyes hurt.

I squinted off to my left and saw the Worm standing there, her pruney lips pinched like they always were, and I couldn't help wondering if I had only imagined her kindness the other day. But then, like she felt someone staring at her, she turned to look at me. She smiled and lifted a hand. I waved back, then the crowd shifted and I couldn't see her anymore.

The Worm. Mrs. Wermer. She'd said a lot of things that afternoon without saying much at all. *You don't have to be like your mother.* And I didn't. I didn't have to make the same mistakes. I didn't have to get pregnant at sixteen, drop out of school, never go to college, never get married. I could be as different from Miracle as I wanted to be.

"Come on," I said, pulling Jenna through the crowd.

"Where are we going?" she shrieked. When she saw I was heading into the square, squeezing through the barricades they had put up to keep the people away, she hollered, "We're not allowed in here!"

"Climb a tree!" I shouted over the roar of chain saws and bulldozers. "Any tree. And don't come down!"

She pulled her hand free. "I can't! My parents will kill me."

"Then do what you think is right."

Not waiting to find out what that would be, I raced over to the tree Miracle had camped out in. I jumped and grabbed the lower branch, swinging myself up. Then I climbed like a monkey. And kept going till I landed on the fort's platform. All of Miracle's things were still there.

Down below I heard shouting, then more shouting, and over it all the whine of chain saws vibrated the air. When I'd caught my breath, I peered over the edge of the fort. Through the leafy branches I saw Jenna struggling up the tree next to mine. I cheered.

Then something else caught my eye. Andrew Pike was climbing one tree over! I couldn't see much else, and it wasn't until later that I found out at least five other kids had broken through the barriers and climbed trees before the police were able to stop them.

One by one, the chain saws and big machinery were turned off. They couldn't cut any more trees down with children in the area. We had stopped progress!

Mayor White, his face red as a kerchief, stood below my tree. When I looked down, he glowered up at me.

"Young lady, come out of that tree this instant," he shouted.

"I can't," I called back.

"You can't, or you won't?" Mayor White demanded.

"I can't. I can't let you cut down all these beautiful old trees."

Reporters had now gotten past the barricades and crowded around the mayor and my tree, aiming cameras and microphones in my direction.

"Just wait till I get your parents here, young lady," the mayor fumed.

I grinned. Obviously he didn't recognize me from up here. *"Parent,"* I said. "My mother is Miracle Bott."

It took a second for the mayor to get it, then his face turned even redder. A couple of men and a woman huddled around the mayor and they talked for a long time, arms jerking, shoulders shrugging, and heads twitching this way and that. I didn't know what they were talking about, and I really didn't care.

I moved away from the edge of the platform and lay back, looking up into the leaves that seemed to dance with happiness in the warm breeze. There were no stars to guide me, but I didn't need them. I would stay up here in the oak as long as I had to, I decided. I didn't want the trees to be cut down. Maybe I wouldn't be able to save any of them. But I'd try my hardest.

I thought of Jenna in the next tree over. Jenna's parents would be angry, or maybe they'd be glad she believed in something enough to climb a tree no matter what. I knew at least that Miracle would be happy and proud for what I'd done. But I hadn't done it for her. I'd done it for me. And if someday I ended up more like Miracle than I ever wanted to, that would be okay.

Memaw might say I'd gotten myself up a creek just like Miracle, but I knew I'd brought my paddle with me. I also knew that I needed Miracle as much as Memaw did. But they needed me, too.

I took my father's phone number out of my pocket. The slip of paper looked like a leaf. I could call Jimmy Wallace, see if he wanted a thirteen-year-old daughter. See if hearing his voice made him my father.

Slowly I tore the piece of paper into tiny flakes, and I put the flakes back into my pocket. I didn't want to litter.

I rolled sideways and gently pulled Miracle's notebook closer to me. She had left it open with a pen marking the page. It was a poem. She must have just finished it when I interrupted her and she fell out of the tree.

It was called "Baby Mine, a Woman Now." I took my time reading it, then read it again even slower. Some parts were funny. Some sad. And more than anything Miracle could have said to me, this poem showed me she understood.

I closed the notebook and thought about the folded triangle of paper I had hidden under Mama's pillow while she was in the bath. The poem I'd written just for her. Some parts were funny. Some sad. And somehow I just knew she'd love it.